HER WICKED LONGING

LAUREN SMITH

Copyright © 2017 by Lauren Smith

Edited by Noah Chinn

Excerpt from *Wicked Designs* by Lauren Smith

Cover art by Erin Dameron-Hill

Scene Art Illustration by Joanne Renaud

Romance Art by Theresa Sprekelmeyer

The League of Rogues (R) is an officially registered Federal Trademark owned by Lauren Smith.

ISBN: 978-1-947206-00-7 (e-book edition)

ISBN: 978-1-947206-01-4 (print edition)

For Amanda,
You have been an inspiration to me and my dearest friend.

FOREWORD

Dear Reader,

Sometimes a story must start in a very particular place and that means that some scenes are left out. Before I ever started to write Audrey or Gillian's stories, I had a sudden and (hopefully you will agree) wonderful idea to tell two short stories that would lead up to Gillian and Audrey's full length adventures. So these two stories are not deleted scenes, nor were they left out of Audrey and Gillian's books but I feel like these two stories had to be told.

These two short stories will show you what a lady and her maid got up to in the day leading up to their adventures when they decide to infiltrate a hellfire club. So please forgive me for these stories end on a note of uncertainty, but rest assured, Audrey and Gillian will have their happy endings with Jonathan and James in their full length books: *His Wicked Secret* and *The Earl of Pembroke* which come out in 2018.

HIS WICKED MAID

A SHORT STORY

CHAPTER 1

Gillian Beaumont knew the day was bound to be full of trouble. As she worked to tame the curls of her mistress's hair, she fretted over the wicked gleam in Audrey Sheridan's eyes. Gillian was used to this mischievous glint, but today it seemed doubly intense, and the way her lips curled at the ends in a little smile added to Gillian's worry even more. The last time she had looked that way, Audrey had been chasing a rogue around a sofa, demanding to be kissed.

"There you are, my lady." Gillian finished putting the last pin in her mistress's hair.

Audrey's brown eyes twinkled as she met Gillian's gaze in the mirror. "Perfect. I have to look my best today. The League is coming over for tea in an hour and…" A delicate blush bloomed in her cheeks.

"And Mr. St. Laurent will be there?"

"Er… I suppose so," Audrey replied vaguely.

Gillian was all too aware of how her mistress felt about that particular gentleman. He was a fine man with green eyes and sun-kissed blond hair. Gillian supposed he was attractive, but he never made her feel the way she'd heard women ought to feel around a man they fancied.

Gillian glanced at her own face in the mirror as she tidied up the vanity. Perhaps she was different from other ladies. She placed the ivory-handled brushes next to a set of exquisite tortoiseshell combs. Unlike Audrey's dark chestnut hair, Gillian's hair was an unremarkable brown and her eyes a soft heather gray. She'd never stood out as a beauty, but she wasn't unattractive, either. She was, in short, the perfect sort of plain woman who worked best as a lady's maid or a companion.

As the bastard daughter of an earl, Gillian had been taught not to expect much of her circumstances, though her father had provided enough for her and her mother. They had lived comfortable if unassuming lives in a little townhouse near Mayfair. When she was fifteen, her father died and she'd been forced into service to support her ailing mother. She'd had no real experience as a companion, but she'd heard from a friend of her mother's that Viscount Sheridan was searching for a lady's maid for his youngest sister, someone close to her in age.

It was unusual to have a lady's maid so young, but Audrey had insisted her maid be close in age. And that was how Gillian, almost sixteen by then, had become Audrey's maid and loyal, protective shadow. A year later, Gillian's mother had passed away.

Now Mama is gone, and I'm all alone.

She frowned. That wasn't true. In many ways, being lady's maid to Audrey was a bit like being Audrey's friend. They shared secrets and went on far too many adventures for Gillian to feel comfortable about. There was a familiarity between them that certainly wasn't normal for a maid and a lady. Audrey had a large heart and a spirit that could not be caged.

"Gillian, could you run a few errands for me today? I believe we have a few articles to post in the *Quizzing Glass Gazette* that will need to run in the next few weeks. Would you mind seeing to that for me?" Audrey was plucking at the waist of her blue cambric muslin gown, where it was fitted perfectly to her trim waist. The dress had ornamented designs on the bodice. Her dress's style and its high waist made Audrey's tiny body look longer. The full skirt was trimmed with lavender gauze that made it look light and almost feathery at the hem.

Audrey had exquisite taste, something she'd insisted her maid cultivate as well. Gillian wore a lavender muslin gown with more flair than a usual lady's maid would wear. It was close in style to the gowns she'd worn when her father was alive.

"Well? Do you mind very much?" Audrey's voice pulled Gillian out of her thoughts.

"Of course, my apologies, my lady. I was woolgathering. Yes, leave me the articles, and I will see them placed in the proper hands."

"Excellent." Audrey walked over to her escritoire and withdrew three carefully packed articles and handed them to Gillian.

"Do you need anything else, my lady?" Gillian asked.

"Not at the moment. Oh, and remember, tonight we will be going to that hellfire club."

Gillian froze midstep, her spine stiffening. The hellfire club, how had she forgotten?

"My lady, I really don't think we should—"

Audrey tapped a dainty foot and crossed her arms over her chest. "Gillian, you know that awful Gerald Langley belongs to that club. What was it called?" Audrey tilted her head, looking up as she seemed to search her memory. "Sinners and Sadists, no... Wait!" She lifted a finger in the air. "The Unholy Sinners of Hell."

Gillian flinched. "Must we go tonight? The men could be dangerous." It wasn't as though their lives were free of gossip and trouble, what with Audrey's elder brother, Cedric, being a member of the infamous League of Rogues. Cedric and his friends had been in life-threatening situations more than once and caused scandals at least every other week. The last thing Audrey needed was to run off and find more trouble—at least that was Gillian's opinion.

"Nonsense. We should be perfectly fine. They allow ladies to attend their unholy festivities, and if we bring along Charles and his valet as escorts, we shall be quite safe."

"Lord Lonsdale? He's not exactly a man of sterling reputation. You remember the swans. Everyone was so scandalized."

Audrey giggled. "Of course I do. I was there. Charles isn't so bad. I had a bloody hard time trying to kiss him, you remember. He's more of a gentleman than he lets on."

With a little hum that wasn't exactly agreement, Gillian headed for the door, but Audrey stopped her.

"The dresses! I completely forgot. You must go to Madame Ella's and retrieve the gowns. Try them on to make sure they fit," Audrey said.

Gillian sighed and nodded. It wasn't the first time she had been asked to try on one of Audrey's gowns. They were almost identical in stature, both short and full-figured. She suspected her mistress was trying to give her a little thrill of pleasure, but Gillian feared longing for things she could never have.

From the moment she'd grown old enough to understand her place as an illegitimate child to a member of the peerage, she'd stopped oohing over the prettiest gowns and had given up dreams of finding a nice gentleman to marry. The acceptance of her fate as a domestic servant had been wearying, and while she adored working for Audrey, even when they were knee-deep in trouble, it didn't stop her from wishing for a quiet life in a little cottage somewhere.

"Thank you." Audrey gently shoved her into the hall, and Gillian headed down the stairs to find her bonnet and coin purse. By the time she finished her errands, the League of Rogues and their wives would have arrived for tea, and Audrey would have little chance of getting into trouble.

Gillian smiled at Sean Hartley, the handsome young Irish footman, as he handed her a small coin purse.

"And what errands does our lady have you running today?" Sean asked, his Irish lilt and fine looks a temptation to all the upstairs maids in the Sheridan residence.

"I'm to collect a few dresses and a few items need to be posted. Could you have the carriage brought around for me?"

Sean grinned. "More dresses. One would think she has enough," he teased and winked at Gillian.

Gillian smiled back. "One would think." She liked Sean. He was like an older brother, playful and kind.

He left her alone in the hall as he summoned a coach. She clutched her purse and the *Gazette* articles to her chest, making sure she wouldn't drop either by accident. No one was around to see, which was good because Sean knew the truth of Audrey's double life. He could be trusted, but neither Audrey nor Gillian wanted to risk anyone else knowing.

It was her lady's best-kept secret. The infamous, sometimes overly critical pen of Lady Society, the anonymous social columnist for the *Quizzing Glass Gazette*, was none other than Audrey Sheridan. Gillian's mistress had written articles for years now, challenging gentlemen to fall in love and publicly exposing those in society who sought to harm others, but her favorite pastime was matchmaking for the rogues she held dear.

Her latest victory had been exposing the betting book at White's, where a man named Gerald Langley had offered five thousand pounds to have a woman publicly ruined. But Audrey wasn't finished with him yet; she had every intention of exposing Langley's involvement in the hellfire club.

And I must go along with it, or else she will get herself into real trouble. Gillian shook her head, tempted to laugh. Was she always to be the voice of reason? It was exhausting keeping her mistress out of trouble time and again. What Audrey truly needed was a man to chase after her and keep her out of harm's way while she led her life of adventures. A man like Jonathan St. Laurent. Once Audrey was married, Gillian would have an ally in her mistress's husband, and she could finally relax.

Sean returned and opened the front door of the townhouse for her.

"Don't worry—I'll keep an eye on her," Sean promised.

"Thank you." Gillian meant it. She worried, as did all the servants, that Audrey would get into a scrape she could not get out of if they did not look after her. Gillian climbed into the coach, settled back, and closed her eyes briefly. She would be facing a long night ahead if they were to infiltrate the hellfire club after midnight.

By the time she reached Madame Ella's modiste shop, she had rested and successfully dropped off the Lady Society articles to their publisher. She felt refreshed and ready to deal with the dress fittings for Audrey. Knowing her lady, it could take a while if the gowns were elaborate, and they were always elaborate.

She had the driver wait for her while she entered the shop. A matronly woman with silver-gray hair was kneeling by a young woman who was wearing a rose-silk gown. The young woman seemed to be around Audrey and Gillian's age of nineteen. She had light-brown hair, professionally styled, and smiled pleasantly at Gillian, assuming by her clothes that she was likely a young woman in a similar social circle.

Madame Ella glanced up and smiled. "Miss Beaumont! What a treat. I have the dresses, but you will need to try them both to be sure." The dressmaker knew Gillian would try on gowns when Audrey could not come herself.

"Of course." Gillian crossed the shop and set her things down in a small curtained area, then took the two gowns from Madame Ella. She quickly removed her own walking dress and tried on her simply tailored evening gown first. It had buttons up the front and was easily examined in the narrow mirror of the small fitting area. But Audrey's evening gown required assistance to be laced up in the back.

"Madame Ella?" she called out. "I need assistance with the laces."

The curtain moved, and she turned halfway, glanced over her shoulder, and gasped. A handsome man with dark hair and soft brown eyes was staring at her, his lips parted. He held a pair of fawn gloves in his hands but didn't move. Her partially unlaced back was exposed to his view. His eyes traced the length of her bared spine, and she could almost feel his gaze, like invisible fingers tiptoeing down her skin.

It made her feel dizzy to know he was seeing her like this, exposed and vulnerable in such a sensual way. His lips curved, just showing a hint of what he must be thinking about as he swept her again from head to toe. Gazing into his brown eyes, she felt like she was falling into an abyss of dark, erotic thoughts. A small voice in the back of her mind warned her she was in dangerous territory. If she'd been a lady like Audrey, she could have been compromised by this.

"My apologies." The man recovered and averted his gaze, his cheeks turning a ruddy red. Gillian's face flushed as well. Yet she still couldn't find her voice to speak. When she stared up at the tall, dark-haired stranger, she simply couldn't *think*. Her heart fluttered wildly, and her stays were suddenly too tight.

"James?" A feminine voice called out. "Where are you? I would like to see if the gloves match this gown."

James, her handsome stranger, half smiled at her and then slowly lowered the hand holding up the curtain. Right before his face vanished from view, his eyes locked on hers, and with a cocky grin he whispered, "Never be ashamed to show such lovely skin."

The curtain fell back into place, and it was as though Gillian could suddenly breathe again. She clutched her arms to her chest, her breasts heaving. She tried to calm down. Who was he? Why hadn't he dropped the curtain at once? Surely he knew how scandalous he'd been.

"Miss Beaumont? Are you ready for me to help with the lacing of the gown?" Madame Ella called outside of the curtain.

"Yes, please come in," she replied, her tone breathless. The dressmaker came inside and made quick work of the laces.

"Well, how does it fit?" Madame Ella asked. Gillian hastily studied the gown and nodded at the dressmaker.

"This will do. Thank you, Madame Ella." She tried desperately to collect her thoughts. Would she see him in the shop again? If he had been assisting a woman buying gloves, they were likely already gone, since she had taken her time finishing trying on Audrey's gown. She hoped he was gone so she wouldn't have to face him, yet she also didn't want him to be gone. The two feelings pulled her in opposite directions. She redressed in her lavender gown and left the dressing room. Her slipper caught on the carpet, and she stumbled.

"Oh!" Gillian gasped, bracing herself for a fall, but instead she fell right into a hard masculine chest. Gentle hands curled around her waist, holding her. The man grasped her more firmly and she was lifted slightly up and into his arms, so that she pressed fully against him. The enticing scent of sandalwood and pine filled her nose, and she raised her head to stare up at the man.

Him.

The handsome mystery man named James. His brown eyes were warm and bright. Her stomach gave a fluttery flip.

"My apologies again." James chuckled and hesitated a moment before he released her waist.

"James? What are you doing?" It was the pretty brunette woman Gillian had seen when she first entered the shop.

"Letty." James greeted her warmly and stepped away from Gillian, but only enough to allow the other woman to come closer to them both.

"Hello." Letty smiled at Gillian. "Don't tell me my older brother was bothering you? He swore to be on his best behavior today. Not that I believed him for a minute. He's a bit of a rogue, you see. Trouble follows him about." Letty's eyes were the same enchanting brown as her brother's. Gillian hated to admit she was relieved they were siblings and not...

It shouldn't matter, but it does.

"No, he's fine. I mean, he was behaving..." A fresh wave of heat and embarrassment swept through her. She usually didn't speak to ladies, not like this.

"I seem to be disrupting the day of Miss..." James looked expectantly to Gillian, clearly hoping she would give him her name. It wasn't proper, this sort of introduction, but at this point *nothing* between them had been proper.

"Beaumont. Gillian Beaumont." The late Earl of Morrey had been Richard Beaumont, but though she bore her father's surname, one would not make the connection or guess that she had been born on the wrong side of the blanket. There were plenty of Beaumonts in London who had no relation to the Morrey title.

"It is a pleasure to meet you, Miss Beaumont. I'm Leticia Fordyce, and this is my brother James, Lord Pembroke."

Gillian nearly swallowed her tongue. *The Earl of Pembroke.* She'd heard the whispers of Audrey's friends over tea, speaking of this man with a wicked smile and gentle brown eyes. He was a mixture of roguish fantasy and perfect gentleman. An enigma the ladies of the *ton* couldn't puzzle out. And yet no one had won his heart. He was just the sort of man she would have longed to dance with at a ball, a man she might have had a chance with if her mother had been married to the Earl of Morrey and not a mistress. But that life would never be hers, and she had to stop thinking about what might have been.

Gillian struggled to think. "It's lovely to meet you both," she managed finally.

What would Audrey Sheridan do? Gillian knew exactly what Audrey would do, and it was not what she would do.

"So, my brother is disrupting your day?" Letty grinned, a little impish smile curling her cupid's bow mouth as she glanced between them.

James stared down at his boots before he glanced up at Gillian, a sheepish grin drawing her focus to his lips. The man had such kissable-looking lips. She jolted. She rarely allowed herself to think of men like that. Her life had always been focused on work and keeping busy. Surviving in London meant abandoning thoughts of marriage. No man would take a penniless illegitimate woman to wife, at least no one above her station.

"I believe Lord Pembroke was looking for you, and I stumbled into him," Gillian replied, trying not to let her nerves show. She wasn't accustomed to speaking directly with members of the peerage.

"Ah." Letty giggled. "We are finished with Madame Ella. Are

you as well? I thought we might go to Gunter's for some ices. Would you care to join us?"

Letty's expression was so full of hope that Gillian's heart twinged with guilt. She had to say no. She couldn't go to Gunter's, not with the earl and his sister. It simply wasn't done. They had mistaken her for a gentle-born lady like Audrey.

She struggled for an excuse. "I regret I must go to a bookshop and pick up a few novels."

"Oh..." Letty's face fell, but James's brown eyes gleamed as he stared at Gillian.

"We are in need of novels too, aren't we, Letty? We shall accompany you, and once we have satisfied our literary thirst, we can quench our physical thirst at Gunter's with tea and ices." The earl declared his plan with such determination that Gillian could not see how she could refuse him.

"I suppose that would be fine..." Living a small lie for a few hours couldn't hurt, could it?

"Wonderful! Did you bring a coach, Miss Beaumont? We have one and would be delighted to take you home after Gunter's if you wish to spare your driver the time," Letty offered.

"Oh no, that's all right. I will have him go to Gunter's and wait for me," Gillian said. If they were to drop her off at the Sheridan townhouse on Curzon Street, it would not take him long to figure out who she really was. She couldn't bring herself to face them should they discover her deception. If she could keep up the pretense for a short while, all would be well.

I should not be doing this...but Audrey doesn't need me this after-noon, and it will be nice to pretend for a few hours. This might have been my life under different circumstances. It was quite selfish to say yes to this madness, she knew, but she was fascinated by James and liked his sister. Surely one visit to a bookshop and Gunter's wouldn't do her any harm. Surely...

CHAPTER 2

J ames Fordyce was under a spell. It was as though some enchantress had stepped into Madame Ella's dress shop and cast a glittering web of light over him. The moment he accidentally pulled back the dressing room curtain and saw her, it was as though no other woman had ever existed before or after in his mind. He was an admitted rogue who'd done things that would make his father blush were the man still alive, yet this woman had made him feel like a lad of seventeen, giddy and gawkish as he gazed at her like a moon-eyed calf.

He'd lost all rational thought when he glimpsed her bare shoulders and back. Pale creamy skin was exposed by the open gown from her neck down to just above a delightfully rounded derrière. He'd had to restrain his baser instincts to grip her hips and pull her back against him.

Once he'd caught sight of those soft gray eyes, he was lost. They were as pale as morning mist covering a field of bluebells. When he gazed deep into her eyes, he had the strangest feeling he was floating somewhere in the clouds, that time seemed to suspend itself and he didn't need to think or breathe outside this single moment. No one had ever made him feel that way before.

Something about this woman filled him with a wild compulsion to strip her of her clothes and possess her right there in the modiste's shop. How was this possible?

At the last moment, he dimly recalled that he was a gentleman, and seeing her in such a way could ruin the lovely gentle-bred lady.

Gillian Beaumont.

A lovely name for a lovely woman. Her face was not what most men might consider that of a typical beauty, but there was something honest and enchanting about her eyes and the openness of her expression. So many women of the *ton* hid their true selves, but not Miss Beaumont. And he'd had the good fortune to have Letty with him to convince the lady to accompany them to Gunter's. If he could claim only a few hours with this woman, he would. As he escorted his sister and Miss Beaumont out of the shop, he wanted to skip about like a young lad.

"Let me carry those." He collected the clothing boxes from Miss Beaumont's arms and escorted her to her coach. It gave him a chance to admire the sway of her hips and the flutter of her lavender skirts as she walked away to inform her driver to wait for her at Gunter's Tea Shop.

"I hope you're bringing home that dark-purple gown, the one I saw you trying on." James teased, and he hoped it wouldn't make her hop in her coach and flee.

"I..." She blushed prettily, and he couldn't help but dream about where else she might blush once he had her beneath him in a bed. The thought made his body rigid with need, but he buried it, which took a lot of effort.

"Well, did you?" He grinned at her as he handed the boxes to the coach driver who secured them in trunks at the back.

She nodded. "It was already fitted. I just had to be sure." Her reply was so methodical he wanted to laugh. She didn't sound like any lady he'd ever met. Most of them wouldn't think about gowns so practically. They would instead gush over the cut of the décolletage or the embroidery on the hem.

"I'm glad it did. I hope to see you wearing it soon. Such a lovely gown will draw the attention of every man in a ballroom."

Her head ducked, and those lovely cheeks stayed bright red. "I suppose it will."

Something about her tone seemed wistful. He cocked his head to one side. Surely she would wear the gown and not let it sit idle in a wardrobe. That would be a travesty.

Once they had returned to his conveyance, he opened the carriage door for the ladies. As he bent his head to pull himself into the coach, he saw Letty making a show of piling her dress boxes next to her, her voice almost trilling as she discussed how much she liked her recent purchases.

James hid a grin at the perceptiveness and playfulness of his sister in realizing he would wish to sit next to Miss Beaumont. He would have to find a way to thank her later, because at the moment he had to take the only available seat—next to his new acquaintance, who spared him a glance of surprise before moving to the far side of the bench. James sat down, flashing a smile in her direction as he allowed his left knee to fall ever so slightly towards her, bumping her lightly. It was impossible not to relish the color in her cheeks. The lady had great restraint and did not pull away from him.

When they entered the bookshop, he was greeted with the pleasant musty smell of old paper and leather. Afternoon peeped through the curtains at the front of the shop, making the spines with gilded lettering gleam and wink. He'd always adored reading, and his own library at his country estate was extensive. He glanced toward Miss Beaumont, and she was staring about at the shop with the same hunger and appreciation for literature he felt. She seemed to sense his focus, and her eyes darted to his.

"A lover of books?" he asked softly.

"Yes, most definitely. How about you, Lord Pembroke?" she replied, her eyes finally settling on him.

"Most definitely," he echoed. "Books feed the dreams and minds of men and women alike. A person who doesn't love books isn't a person worth knowing."

"I quite agree. If you don't read, you often have so little of worth to say in conversation," she added.

"Well," Letty said with a chuckle. "I see you two will be fine if I leave you for a few minutes. The shopkeeper must help me find the book I'm looking for." She made herself scarce in a distant part of the store where she could not be seen. James wanted to crow in triumph. His sister was most certainly playing match-maker, and he couldn't have been more delighted. She'd chased off more than one lady who'd attempted to catch his eye, but she seemed to like Miss Beaumont.

James escorted Miss Beaumont farther into the bookshop. "Where may I escort you? Perhaps the latest in sciences, or the philosophy section, or the newest novels?"

"The novels, if you please." Her blue-gray eyes held a faint twinkle that gave him hope he might yet win her with his teasing.

"Novels? This way." He took her through a few more crowded aisles, not having the faintest clue where to find the novels, but he did his best to look about purposefully, until she started to giggle.

"Do you even know where the novels are?" She covered her mouth with a gloved hand to hide her smile.

"Er... Not in this particular shop..." He stopped and then glanced around. "Aha!" He pointed to a gilded sign that hung above the nearest shelf. It read, "Novels."

"You were lucky," Miss Beaumont said, giggling.

"Ahem." He straightened his shoulders. "What sort of novels are you searching for, Miss Beaumont?"

His teasing tone was rewarded by a smile that curved her lips as she studied the shelves of books around them. "I'm afraid you will judge me harshly if I admit it."

"Nonsense. I would never judge a lady, especially a beguiling one." Was that a coquettish tilt to her head as she flicked a gaze his way? James pressed on, crossing his index finger over his heart in a childlike way.

She laughed, though her eyes glanced away from his before raising to meet them again. "Very well." She lifted her chin. "I rather enjoy gothic novels. L. R. Gloucester has a new book out. *Lady Gloria and the Earnest Earl.*"

Castles, supernatural forces, and dire stakes were something that delighted her? James couldn't fault her for that; he had a fondness for such things as well.

"I've read one or two of those. Most amusing, if I do say so. Towers and storms and passionate affairs. It's exciting, isn't it?" He trailed a fingertip along the shelf nearest him, tapping the spine of each book as he walked.

"It is," Miss Beaumont admitted. "What do you enjoy reading, Lord Pembroke?"

"Well..." He paused to think as they both studied the titles stacked neatly on the shelves. "I like a bit of everything. It's good to be well versed in many things, but I suppose I like a bit of poetry most, aside from novels."

"Poetry?" Miss Beaumont's blue-gray eyes grew wide. "Most gentlemen of my acquaintance have no patience for poetry."

"A pity for them. Poetry is a window to a person's soul. With just a few words, a great writer can move mountains. I read it when I need to find a place of strength." He realized he was revealing far more of himself to this woman than he had intended to.

"And who do you read that gives you strength?" she asked.

"John Donne. A bit old-fashioned, I know, but there's something about him..."

Miss Beaumont lingered close to the shelf, her eyes drifting as she recalled a passage by Donne.

. . .

Let maps to others, worlds on worlds have shown,
    Let us possess one world, each hath one, and is one.

His shock was momentary as he recognized Donne's "The Good-Morrow," and he couldn't help but reply.

If our two loves be one, or thou and I
    Love so alike that none do slacken, none can die.

She shivered, and he felt it too, a wildness that skittered beneath his skin until it created a lingering sense of chills along his arms and the back of his neck. How alike they were, and how strange he had never met her before now. How was it possible? He'd met nearly every woman in London of marriageable age, from debutantes to aging spinsters. But he had never once glimpsed this beauty from across a ballroom.

"Sometimes it is nice to escape one's daily life, don't you agree?" Miss Beaumont asked.

Escape her daily life? James couldn't help but wonder what about her daily life was poor enough that she longed for escape. Then again, he'd heard Letty often complain about what little women had to do during a day. Shopping, riding, paying calls, the dreaded embroidery hoop... Perhaps Miss Beaumont found it tedious as well. His esteem grew for this quiet, intelligent beauty.

"Er... Yes. I feel that way too." It was true enough. Sometimes he wished he was happily married and settled down, but his duties to his title and his estate rarely let him have a moment for himself. One of his few indulgences was belonging to a rather elite underground gathering known as the Wicked Earls' Club. Aside from his time spent at the club, he did his best to behave himself.

"Ah." Gillian paused in front of him and used a gloved fingertip to pull a book out of its shelf and examine the title page. "Found it."

James plucked the book from her hands, delighting in her little gasp as she tried to take it back.

"Oh please, give it back!" She lunged for it, and he danced out of reach. When she gave up, he grinned and skimmed through the first few pages.

"Well, this chap doesn't waste any time. Listen to this." He chose a passage, speaking in a deep baritone, pretending to be the hero. "Lady Gloria lay prostrate on the bed, listening to the sounds of rain on the gables and dreading the moment her captor, the Earl of Blackacre, would come. When he'd kissed her in the corridor only one hour before, their passionate embrace had promised dark, delicious things, and she'd been unable to resist him..." James trailed off, his words ending in a silken whisper.

Miss Beaumont had stopped trying to reach for the book, their bodies mere inches apart, her face tilted up to his. An energy rippled through him to her in that moment. Her face was a delightful rosy red, and her lips were parted in shock.

"Shall I continue?" he asked, stepping closer. He was damn tempted to steal a kiss, no matter how scandalous it would be.

CHAPTER 3

Gillian couldn't breathe. James was reading a torrid part of a novel in public, and she was mortified...and she didn't want him to stop. It had nothing to do with the story and everything to do with his hypnotic voice. Her heart was racing, and she could only stare at James's lips in utter fascination. So this was what it felt like to long for a man—and it was indeed a longing...a wicked one.

"Shall I continue?" he asked again, moving closer. Gillian glanced around the little bookshop. They had wandered into a dim corner as they talked where no one could see them. Her heart gave another wild set of beats as she licked her lips nervously.

"You shouldn't do that," he cautioned her gently as he closed the book and set it on the shelf ledge by his hip.

"Do what?" She tried to back up, but her bottom hit a shelf behind her.

"Lick your lips. It makes a man wonder how you taste, how you feel..." He reached up, cupped her cheek, and stroked the pad of his thumb over her bottom lip. The touch burned in the most delicious way.

21

"Lick my..." She processed his words and then gasped.

James chuckled. "I'm trying to be a gentleman, but Lord you are tempting me." He lifted her chin up and then lowered his head until their mouths were inches apart.

"I fear that if you do not demand for me to step away, I will kiss you." His voice was strained, his brown eyes rich and warm. Staring into them made her feel dizzy, and her body felt languid, as though she had lain beneath the summer sun in a bed of cool grass for hours.

"Kiss me?" The words escaped as a question, but James didn't seem to consider them as such.

"Hmmm, if you insist," he murmured softly. An instant before their lips met, her eyes closed, and she melted against him when his mouth touched hers. He kissed like an angel, all fire and sweetness with a hint of wickedness where his tongue traced the seam of her lips. She jolted in surprise and her lips parted, allowing him to slip his tongue between them. He opened his mouth over hers, and she moaned at the delicious feeling of being helpless in the wake of the heated passion sweeping through her. She could feel the faintest scrape of the stubble on his chin against her skin, and it burned deliciously as he nuzzled her neck.

This was how a lady was ruined. This was the glory they risked so much for. She'd never understood her mistress's yearning for love and marriage and a man...until now.

James cupped her face, his thumb stroking her cheek as he gazed down at her in wonder and fascination. "Why can't I resist you, Miss Beaumont?"

"I don't know." She blinked, dazed by the fact that she and the Earl of Pembroke were pressed chest to chest against the bookshelf.

"Have you ever felt like this before?" he asked.

"No, never. I was beginning to worry something might be wrong with me." She half laughed, but the sound was tremulous. She shouldn't have confessed that—a lady wouldn't have.

But you're not a lady, her inner voice reminded her sharply. *You're a servant, and he believes you are gentle-born.*

"Have you kissed many other men?" James's question was full of curiosity and a hint of jealousy.

"No, but then, I've never wanted anyone to kiss me before," she explained in a scandalized whisper. The simple curve of his lips made her smile too.

"Good. The thought of you with another man might drive me mad."

Worry creased her brows. "Are you a jealous sort of man?"

James shook his head. "Never. But you make me feel different."

He didn't seem to know what else to say, and she didn't want to speak, either. She bit her bottom lip and peered up at him from beneath her lashes. She couldn't be as bold as Audrey, but she hoped he would take her actions as an invitation.

He did. He curled his arm around her waist and brought her back into his arms. She placed her palms on his waistcoat and curled her fingers into his lapels as their lips met in another fiery kiss. He moved his mouth over hers, and she couldn't help but moan at the way he made her feel, on fire everywhere. No wonder Audrey was chasing rogues about, begging for kisses. If they all felt like this, she could understand.

"James? James? Where are you?" Letty's voice carried through the shelves, and he hastily stumbled back from Gillian just before his sister found them. She held a trio of historical volumes and was watching them curiously.

"Did Miss Beaumont find her book?"

"Er... Yes." James held out the book, and Gillian tried not to laugh at the almost boyish guilt written on his face. Letty was younger than her brother, and it was clear James tried to be on his best behavior around her, as though striving to please her. The notion was charming. It reminded Gillian of her mistress's older brother, Cedric, Viscount Sheridan. Despite being a notorious rogue, he was impossibly sweet to his sisters.

"Excellent." Letty grinned at her. "James, would you buy these for me?" She shoved the stack of books into his chest. He fumbled as he clutched at them. "I want to talk with Miss Beaumont."

James's eyes twinkled as he looked at them. "You wish to talk about matters of a feminine nature, I assume?" He held Letty's books and began to turn around, but then Gillian caught his arm.

"Oh, you have mine. I shall need to pay as well."

"Nonsense. I'll buy it for you." He tucked the book firmly between two of Letty's where Gillian could not reach it.

"Oh, please, I really must insist." Gillian made another valiant effort to reach for the book, but James *tsked* and shook his head.

"Consider it a gift from me for a delightfully unexpected change in my day. If you hadn't been at the modiste, Letty would've spent all day trying on bonnets." James rolled his eyes, and Letty pretended to pout. Before Gillian could argue, James vanished with the books, leaving her alone with his sister. She'd been ignoring the truth of her deception for the last hour, but reality had returned once she was out of James's arms.

This isn't my world. I should not be here, letting them both assume I'm one of them. How can they not see? Her hair was simply styled. Her dress, while more fancy than that of a usual lady's maid, was still a servant's dress.

"He is right, you know. I would've stayed there all day. I'm certain he would've perished on Madame Ella's fainting couch waiting for me."

Gillian giggled at the thought of James lying prone on a fainting couch, a ghastly expression on his face, one arm thrown over his eyes in despair while Letty dropped more bonnets on his lap.

"He's a wonderful man, my brother, quite wonderful," Letty said, watching Gillian with a keenness that remind her all too well of her mistress when she was plotting something.

"Er... Yes, I imagine he is," she answered carefully.

Letty studied the books around her, a pensive look upon her face.

"He deserves a good wife, you know. Quite a few ladies have set their caps for him, but…" Letty trailed off. She sighed and met Gillian's confused gaze. "Well, none of them are interested in a love match. I believe my brother deserves that, don't you agree?"

There was a hint of warning in Letty's tone that Gillian understood. If she wouldn't love James, she needed to leave him alone. Which of course she must, because earls didn't marry ladies' maids.

"I agree," she said quietly. "I have no designs upon him, truthfully, Miss Fordyce."

Letty smiled. "If you did think you were developing feelings for him, that would be acceptable." Her answer surprised Gillian.

"But—" she began.

"I want no title hunters for James. It's love or nothing. After our father passed away, our mother grew…forgetful and unwell, and it's up to me to protect him, at least in the ways of the heart."

"A noble endeavor," Gillian agreed. If she'd had siblings to look out for, she would have done the same. She had two half-siblings, a sister and a brother, but… Well, they didn't even know about her, and she could never tell them. She was a bastard child, after all, and a servant.

Letty looked ready to speak again, but James returned, books stacked in his arms.

"Shall we deliver these to the footman? I don't want to be carrying books into Gunter's. They might end up sticky if someone's flavored ice melts."

"Good point, James." Letty, James, and Gillian left the shop. Gillian still couldn't believe she was here on the streets with an earl and his sister, acting the part of a fine lady, but the deception had gone too far, and she could not go back now.

They climbed into the carriage that bore the Pembroke crest

and gave the books to the footman, who tucked them in a leather coach box. When they reached Gunter's, James offered to let them stay in the carriage. The weather was fine, and Gillian and Letty agreed it would be more pleasant to eat their ices in the carriage rather than go indoors where the crowds were sure to be.

Young men, employees of Gunter's, ran across the street to carriages and back again, carrying ices. Letty waved to a few ladies in another carriage and turned to James and Gillian. "It's been positively ages since I've talked with Miss Dawkins and Lady Fairchild. Do you mind if I go and see them?"

"Not at all," James replied before glancing to Gillian, who nodded, but blushed.

It was perfectly acceptable not to be chaperoned at Gunter's. It was one of the few places in London that escaped the stigma of being a place where a lady could be ruined simply by being alone with a man. Letty hastily departed the carriage and went to join her friends. Gillian now sat facing James. A flutter of nerves stirred in her belly, and she resisted the urge to place a hand over her stomach.

"Afraid to be alone with me?" James teased. "We're quite safe here."

Gillian blushed. "I'm not afraid. I've just never been to Gunter's..." *As a lady*, she added silently. She'd followed her mistress there plenty of times, but never to indulge in confectionaries or converse with gentlemen. She was watchful and silent unless her lady needed her.

"Never been to Gunter's? Lord, where have you been, Miss Beaumont?" James leaned forward slightly, resting his forearms on his knees. He studied her curiously.

"Where have I been?" she echoed, confused by his question.

"Clearly you haven't been in London. I mean, if you haven't been to Gunter's."

"Oh..." She scrambled to come up with a story of where she'd been. "I live in the country and rarely come to London." She searched her memory in vain for a place he'd likely not have been to. "I'm from Lothbrook." It was a small village, one she'd never heard of until recently when Audrey had used her influence as the secret columnist Lady Society to reunite a young woman from Lothbrook with a rakehell who'd fallen in love with her.

"Lothbrook," James mused thoughtfully. "Where have I heard that name before?"

"Oh—"

Before Gillian could find herself in deeper trouble, she jumped as a Gunter's employee suddenly appeared by the carriage and held out two dishes with ices inside.

"Thank you." James handed the lad his payment, and when Gillian attempted to argue, he *tsked* and waved a finger at her.

"Miss Beaumont, do you really think a proper gentleman would allow you to pay for your own ices?" The teasing look in his eyes made her flush all over, and she felt bold enough to respond by showing a flare of minor annoyance with him.

"After what occurred in the bookshop, you are claiming to *be* a proper gentleman, Lord Pembroke?"

James dipped his spoon into his ice and took a bite. As he licked his lips, his lashes lowered to half-mast.

"I confess. You've discovered my flaw. I'm more rogue than gentleman, and I don't plan to apologize for that kiss, not when you tasted sweeter than this ice."

Gillian gasped. His openly sensual words were too much.

"I know, I am terribly wicked." A smile touched his lips, the soft intensity of his words making her melt.

"Yes, you are." She tried to sound accusing, but her tone was breathless.

"And you like it," he added quickly.

"Yes, I… Wait, no. I most certainly do not!" She dropped her spoon into the ice dish, scowling at him. This was not right. The devil. A rogue, talking of kisses and sweet tastes with a stranger, a stranger he didn't even know wasn't worthy of his attentions. She covered the rising despair of this with irritation.

"Please finish your ice before it melts and my gentlemanly gesture goes to waste." He used the tip of his spoon to point at her dish.

Gillian stared at the melting ice, and with a little *humph* she finished eating it, all too aware of James watching her. She'd never been so frustrated by a man in her life, nor had she ever been in such an uncomfortable position, either. How could Audrey stand to be around Jonathan when she felt this way? Gillian had a sudden appreciation for her mistress's ability to keep her head around the man she was attracted to.

When she was done, James had an attendant from the store collect the dishes. Then he cast one glance at his sister, who was still deep in conversation with her friends a few carriages away.

"It seems Letty won't be returning anytime soon." James started to move toward Gillian to join her in her seat, but he froze when someone called his name.

"Pembroke? Fancy finding you here." A familiar voice made Gillian tense and glance about.

A handsome gentleman approached their coach on a horse. The fine gelding started as the gentleman tugged lightly on the reins. It was Mr. Ambrose Worthing, the rakehell she and Audrey had helped a few weeks ago in Lothbrook. She liked Mr. Worthing, but he knew she was not a gentle-born lady. She had to say something to stop him from exposing her masquerade.

"Mr. Worthing! It's so good to see you again," she said, meeting his gaze intensely.

Mr. Worthing's lips parted, and it took him a mere moment to catch her silent warning.

"Miss Beaumont. Lovely to see you again as well," he echoed.

"How are you, Worthing?" Pembroke asked with a grin. "You and the wife settled in?"

"Yes, who knew married life would suit me so well?" Mr. Worthing chuckled. "I always thought I'd be dragged to the altar, screaming for help. But once I knew Alexandra was the only woman I could ever love...well, it made marriage a necessity."

James laughed. "It seems like everyone I know is rushing off to get leg-shackled."

"You're not tempted in the slightest?" Mr. Worthing jested, glancing determinedly at Gillian. Her heart leapt into her throat.

James barked out a laugh.

"Perhaps I am a bit tempted." His eyes locked with Gillian's, and she couldn't look away. The honey-fired depths of his eyes seemed to draw her in, trapping her until she forgot where she was and who she was with. Gillian never could have imagined how dangerous a pair of brown eyes could be.

"Well, I can see I am intruding," Mr. Worthing cut in, with a hint of mirth in his tone. "But I'm glad I did meet with you, Miss Beaumont. I have a letter for you." Mr. Worthing reached into his waistcoat and removed a folded bit of parchment. He held it out to Gillian, his gaze serious. She took it. There was no name upon the outside, merely two letters—*LS*—which Gillian knew instantly meant it was intended for Lady Society.

"Thank you, Mr. Worthing." She was about to tuck it into her reticule when Worthing spoke again.

"I'm afraid it's rather urgent." Once again, his eyes were serious.

"Oh!" She fumbled to break the seal. As she took out the letter, she glanced once more at Worthing.

"If you need to reply, send it to my London address," Worthing said. He nodded in farewell to Pembroke, who watched them curiously.

"Thank you." Gillian watched Mr. Worthing dig his heels into his gelding's flanks and ride off. Only then did she unfold the parchment to read the letter.

. . .

My dear LS,

It has been rumored that Gerald Langley seeks to lure you to his hell-fire club tonight. He believes he will at last have the revenge he seeks. I pray, nay, I insist you stay home this evening. You've done Langley enough harm. You need not endanger yourself further.

Yours,

Worthing

Gillian read the words once more, her heart pounding. She'd known tonight's scheme to infiltrate the hellfire club had been a very terrible idea. But she couldn't have imagined it would be so dangerous. She would have to warn her mistress at once.

"Is everything all right, Miss Beaumont? You've gone very pale." James moved to sit beside her.

"Y—yes," she stammered, unnerved by his closeness and the contents of the letter. She jumped when he placed his gloved hand over hers. His palm was warm and his fingers strong, but gentle as they curled around her fingers.

"My lord, you mustn't. People are watching us." She glanced away, wishing she'd worn a bonnet today so she might've hidden her face from searching eyes.

"Let them see. I like you, Miss Beaumont. And I've only known you but a few hours."

Gillian laughed, but the sound was watery. "My lord, you do not know me at all." Her heart clenched. "I am most grateful for everything you've done today, but I'm afraid I really must go."

She pulled her hand free of his, hating how she missed his touch. She'd never thought she would fall for any man, certainly not one like the Earl of Pembroke. It was time to go, to end this silly charade before her heart was truly broken. She climbed out of the carriage, glancing about for her own coach and found it at the end of the street.

"Miss Beaumont, please, let me escort you." James climbed down, trying to take her hand again. Gillian's eyes stung with tears, and she blinked them back. *What is wrong with me? I've never hurt so.* But having to convince James to leave her alone was making her bleed inside.

"Please, my lord. You should remain with your sister." Then, before she could let him convince her to stay, she rushed toward the waiting coach farther down the street.

Just as she reached the coach, a man emerged from the mews between two shops and gripped her arm. Something sharp dug into her side, and she opened her mouth to scream.

"Hush now, pet. I've got a knife, and it's sharp enough to cut you through your stays and make a nice little hole. We wouldn't want that, now would we?" The man was dressed like a gentleman, but the heavy scruff on his jaw and Cockney accent assured her he was no gentleman.

"You're going to be good, aren't you?" the man asked quietly in her ear. "Nod, if you agree."

Gillian nodded her head hesitantly.

"Let's go for a little walk down 'ere." He dragged her into the mews he had just emerged from. There was an open door on the left, leading to rooms above a shop front. Gillian tried to dig in her heels a little as they reached the door, her mouth filled with a strange bitter taste. The knifepoint pricked her, and she couldn't stop the whimper that escaped. Instinct took over, and she wriggled in his hold, wanting to flee the man and his knife.

"Stop fightin' me!" the man snarled and dug one hand into her hair, jerking her head back as he used the painful hold to drag her inside the darkened doorway. She was slammed against the wall, her head striking against wood. She dropped the letter from her reticule. She tried to touch her head.

"Ah... 'Ere we are." The man bent down and grasped the letter. With this temporary distraction, he lowered the knife so that it was close to the floor while he retrieved the letter meant for her mistress. Gillian didn't need the letter, which gave her a chance to use his diverted focus to escape. She scrambled for the door but cried out as the man grabbed her skirts and yanked hard.

She fell to her knees, and something hit her temple. In the blink of an eye, everything went dark.

CHAPTER 4

J ames stood beside his carriage, watching Miss Beaumont
walk away. As the distance between them lengthened, his
heart grew heavier, he realized something had been taken
from him.

She had seemed so lost as she'd pulled away from him. There
had been a glimmer of tears in her eyes that he didn't understand.
He wanted to go after her. There was something wrong—he
sensed it. He would escort her home, even if she protested. Whatever
was in that letter had upset her greatly, and she shouldn't
have to return home alone. James told his driver to wait for Letty
and take her home. He would hire a hackney once he'd seen Miss
Beaumont safely to her residence.

When he turned back to the street, he saw the distant figure of
Gillian as she reached the end of the street. Suddenly, a man came
toward her and grabbed her arm. Panic flared inside him. No
gentleman would grab a lady's arm like that, and out of nowhere,
no less. James frowned. Did she know the man? The intimate
stance indicated that she did, but he was too far to see clearly
what was occurring between them. She and the man turned away
from her coach and walked into the mews, vanishing from view.

The knot of worry in his gut grew stronger. What was she doing? The man seemed off somehow in a way James couldn't place. There was a menace in the way he was moving toward Gillian, and James didn't feel comfortable leaving her alone, her protestations be damned. He began to walk briskly, but after a few seconds he began to run. As he reached the mews, he nearly collided with the man, who cursed at him and stumbled back before he rushed out of the alley.

What—?

There was no sign of Gillian. He scanned the mews, peering deep into the shadows cast by buildings on either side. He squinted and saw a door open farther down the narrow lane. A pale hand was stretched across the floor over the threshold.

"Gillian!" Fear strangled him as he rushed to the door. He skidded to a stop at her side as she lay on the floor.

"Oh Lord," he gasped as he knelt down and turned her over. He placed two fingers against her throat. A steady pulse beat against them. She was alive. He examined her and saw a reddened mark against one temple. The man had struck her!

James knelt down and lifted her up in his arms, cradling her against his chest. She needed to be seen by a physician immediately. He rushed to her coach.

"Excuse me!" he called out to the driver. "Are you Miss Beaumont's coachman?" The driver glanced down and cursed in surprise at what he saw. He rushed from his seat to help James get Gillian inside.

"What happened?" the driver demanded, his eyes scanning Gillian's motionless body.

"Some bloody bastard struck her. She has to be seen by a physician at once."

"Thank you, my lord." The driver helped settle Gillian on the seat.

"I will accompany you. I should not like to leave the lady alone until I'm assured of her well-being."

The driver hesitated, but James crossed his arms over his chest and scowled. "Very well, my lord. Hop in."

James took a seat and then leaned over to lift Gillian onto his lap. The thought of not holding her made him restless and anxious. He brushed a lock of her hair from her eyes and traced his thumb over her lips, hating the fact that the only reason she was in his arms now was because she'd been injured.

"I'm so sorry," he murmured to her.

Gillian suddenly stirred, her head swaying a little as she came around. For a long moment, he couldn't breathe as he watched her eyelashes flutter, and then she was staring up at him.

"Wh—What happened...?" She licked her lips and reached up to touch her head.

"Don't—" He tried to stop her, but she winced as her hand touched the sensitive part of her temple.

"How..." Gillian let out a little cry of pain. It tore at his heart. Seeing her hurt like this was destroying him.

"Be at ease Miss Beaumont, I saw you headed for this coach when you were dragged into the mew by that man. I wasn't able to stop him but I found you. Would you like to sit up?" he asked softly. He didn't want her to leave his arms, but she nodded.

"I should—it's not proper."

He chuckled wryly. "It's a closed coach. No one will see. Besides, you are in distress, and I intend to give any assistance I can."

"Distress?" She snorted. "I'm not some damsel, Lord Pembroke."

"No, of course not." He knew he must have upset her idea of her own feminine strength by implying she was some damsel in distress. She loved to read Gothic novels but clearly had no desire to live in one. He understood. Letty would have struck him with one of her fine fawn gloves if he dared to imply she was in need of rescuing.

Gillian slid off his lap and sat beside him, delicately feeling the area around her reddened temple again.

"What was that man after? He hit you, but he left your reticule behind and didn't seem to want to..." He swallowed down the word *force*. That was a frightening subject for ladies, and he didn't want to frighten her.

"It was the letter he was after. It was important." She sighed, her eyes grave.

"The letter? He has it now?"

She nodded. "Unfortunately, yes. He took it. But he won't learn much. I read it, and that's all that matters." Her fingers trailed over her torn skirts where the man had likely grabbed her.

"What was in the letter, Miss Beaumont?"

"I wish I could tell you, but it's not my secret to share."

James gaped. "Whatever was in that letter almost got you killed, and yet you won't tell me?"

She reached out, touching his knee, her eyes pleading with him. "I wish I could, but I mustn't. I'm so very sorry."

It was madness. What secret could be so dangerous that a gentle-born lady would be unable to tell him?

"Could you take me to the Sheridan townhouse? I must speak with a friend there."

"Lord Sheridan's townhouse? Very well." James sighed and opened the window of the coach door and gave the driver the address.

Once he settled back in his seat, he watched her, careful not to miss her restless shifting as flashes of pain crossed her eyes when she moved her head a certain way.

"Stop moving so much, Miss Beaumont. You likely sprained your neck in the fall."

"Sprained my neck?" She rubbed her neck but couldn't seem to reach the spot that caused her discomfort.

"Would you allow me to help?" he asked gently. He had no

desire to take advantage of her, even if he was a rogue most days. He couldn't stand to see this captivating creature in pain.

"Help how?" Gillian's voice was soft and slightly breathless.

"You'll permit me to touch you?" He lifted his hand to her cheek but didn't touch her until she nodded. This was different than a stolen kiss in the bookstore. She was hurt and alone with him, and she needed to know he would never hurt her.

He reached up and placed his fingers on her shoulders and moved them down to her neck, gently massaging the little knots of tension he found there. He'd had a mistress once who had been very clever at massage and had taught him exactly where to apply pressure.

"That feels wonderful. How did you know it would make the pain ease?"

"It will calm your muscles if you massage them lightly where they have been strained." He trailed his index finger along one taut tendon in her neck, indicating where he would continue to touch her. "Relax. Face away from me. I want you to draw in a deep breath and let it out slowly."

Gillian hesitated for a moment before she tucked up her legs on the seat and offered him her back. He carefully kneaded her neck and shoulders, even rubbing his fingers into her hair at the base of her skull. Her little moan of pleasure made his body tighten with arousal and shame. He promised himself he would be a gentleman for a few minutes longer if he could.

How was this woman so bloody tempting? He could have almost any woman in London, yet this quiet, intense, and mysterious beauty had him enraptured. It had to be the cloak of danger she wore. That was what drew him in. He loved a good adventure.

The coach came to a stop, and the driver called out that they had reached the Sheridan townhouse.

"Thank you, my lord. It feels much better." Gillian turned toward him, and he reluctantly let go of her.

"Miss Beaumont, I really should make sure you see a physician."

She shook her head. "My friend can send for one if I still feel unwell."

Gillian collected her reticule and reached for the door. He beat her to it, opening it for her. She blinked as though she were surprised he would open the door for her. Were there no gentlemen in Lothbrook? He assisted her down, relishing this last chance he had to hold her waist and feel her hands on his shoulders before he had to set her down.

"You are certain you don't wish for me to go inside with you?" he asked, hoping she would change her mind.

"No, please. I must visit my friend in private. The driver will see you home." She started to wave to the coachman and pull a few extra coins from her reticule, but James caught her hand, gently pulling it to his lips for a kiss.

"No need. I believe I could use a walk." There was no doubt he needed to clear his head.

"Thank you, Lord Pembroke. Truly. I do not know what would've happened if you hadn't come after me." Her lips trembled, but she didn't seem to be a weak, delicate creature to him. She was brave, and to have endured what she did with such grace was astonishing.

"May I call upon you?" he asked. The thought of this mysterious woman returning to Lothbrook and never seeing her again made his chest hollow.

"I…" She bit her bottom lip. "I don't think that would be wise." She seemed like she wanted to say more but changed her mind and rushed up the steps. She didn't bother knocking on the door, but burst inside, vanishing from view.

James stood at the bottom step, staring at the lion's head knocker and trying to ignore the odd ache beneath his ribs. Only a few minutes had passed when he began to walk home and realized the book he bought for her was still in his coach with Letty.

~

"Is he gone?" Gillian asked Sean, who was peering discreetly out the window at the sidewalk where she'd left James standing.

"Yes. He's just started to walk down the street. What happened?" The young Irishman looked concerned.

"It's a long story, and I really need to rest a moment. Is Miss Sheridan back?"

"Not yet. The League is in the parlor having tea. Our mistress took one look at Mr. St. Laurent when he arrived and fled the house. Didn't even take her bonnet." Sean chuckled.

"What?" That was certainly unlike Audrey. She never left the house without a proper bonnet. She loved them too much to be seen without one.

"Of course, there was quite a scandal among the staff."

"What? Why?" Gillian followed Sean down the stairs to the servants' kitchens, where she eased into a chair by the fire and stole a biscuit from a tray when the cook had her back turned.

"Well, Mr. St. Laurent sees her go and asks me where she ran off to. I tried to tell him I had no idea, and then he rushed after her. No one has seen either of them since."

"Oh dear..." Gillian rubbed her eyes. Audrey had run off, and St. Laurent had pursued her? That was bound to lead to trouble. "Was Lord Sheridan very concerned?"

The footman blushed. "He doesn't know. He's been busy, you see."

"Busy?" Gillian echoed.

"Yes. Apparently it's not only the Duchess of Essex and the Marchioness of Rochester who are expecting."

"What?" Gillian sat up, her aching head momentarily forgotten as her friend grinned. "Tell me, Sean, what is it?"

"Well, it seems..." The Irishman drew out the suspense until she couldn't stand it. "That Sheridan House will be hearing the cry of a babe in six or seven months. The League take making babes as seriously as they do weddings."

Gillian giggled, pure joy filling her. Lady Sheridan and Lord Sheridan were expecting. What wonderful news!

"So, you can imagine, none of the League are focused on Miss Audrey or Mr. St. Laurent at the moment. In fact, Essex and Rochester were placing bets on which babe would be the stronger chap once the little ones grow up. None of the lords seem to think their firstborns might be wee lassies." Sean put a kettle of water on the stove, ignoring the harrumph of the cook, who liked her kitchen to be free of meddling footmen when she was working hard to prepare dinner. Gillian smiled faintly at the thought of those powerful lords all discussing children. She'd seen those men with their wives, and if the way they acted around the women they loved was any indication, those lords would be wrapped around the delicate fingers of their children once they were born. It was wonderful, simply wonderful to think of children growing up in households full of love and laughter. Not like her own house, which had been quiet and empty save for her mother and a handful of servants. Her thoughts strayed back to James and what Letty had said about his father dying and his mother becoming ill. He too had had a trying life, despite a title and money. It was one more thing they had in common, yet she would never see that man again, no matter how much she might wish to.

"Now, are you ready to tell me what happened today?" Sean leaned down and gently cupped her cheek, turning her face so he could get a better look. "What happened to your face? Did Lord Pembroke—?"

"No." She cut him off before he could assume the worst about the man who had been her champion. "I was hit by a man in an alley, and Lord Pembroke came to my rescue. I'm afraid my head hurts something fierce."

Sean was still scowling. "You're going to tell me everything that happened." He stole a few biscuits, poured her a cup of tea, and sat beside her, listening to her tale of the letter. He was the only one they could trust about Audrey's double life. She left out the glorious kisses from the earl and the fact that she'd spent the afternoon masquerading as a lady. Sean would have disapproved of her deception. When she was finished, the footman was up on his feet, pacing the kitchen, much to the frustration of the cook, who had to keep dodging him as she prepared the evening meal.

"We must find Miss Sheridan at once."

Gillian agreed. Audrey could be in danger. Whoever had attacked her in the alley had wanted the letter, most likely because he was involved in the scheme to track down and harm Lady Society. But Gillian had read the note and knew of the threat. As long as she could find Audrey and warn her in time, they might yet save her.

She followed Sean back up the steps into the main entryway just as the front door flew open. Audrey strode in, her hair down in wild tangles, her cheeks flushed, and her skirts rumpled.

"My lady!" Gillian gasped. Had something happened to her? She'd never seen her mistress so ruffled before except...the night she and Charles had faked a rather rough seduction to pressure Cedric into letting Audrey marry someone and soon. Had Audrey actually been kissing someone to look so...mussed?

"Gillian?" Audrey seemed distracted and a little surprised to see her.

"Yes, my lady." Gillian and Sean both bowed their heads, but Sean spoke up.

"My lady, we must speak with you. I'm afraid it's a matter of urgency."

"Oh?" Audrey waited for them to follow her upstairs to her private study.

Once they were inside with the door closed, Audrey took a seat and looked at them expectantly.

"My lady, you received a warning from Mr. Worthing. You must not go through with tonight's plan."

Audrey's brow furrowed. "But why not? You know those men are monsters. I cannot let them continue their awful meetings."

Gillian's head ached, and she shared a glance with Sean. "My lady, there was a man. He attacked me to get that letter given to me by Mr. Worthing."

"Attacked! Heavens, Gillian, are you all right?" Audrey was on her feet in an instant, rushing to Gillian's side and tugging her into a chair. "Please, sit. I had no idea."

For the first time, Gillian saw genuine concern in her mistress's eyes.

"I'm all right. Lord Pembroke assisted me and escorted me home."

"He did? James is such a dear," Audrey murmured.

A sudden flash of envy shot through Gillian at hearing Audrey speak James's name with open and easy familiarity. It only reminded her of the gulf that separated them.

"I should thank him," Audrey added.

"No!" Gillian gasped. Sean and Audrey stared at her, and she knew she would have to explain, at least in part, the rest of her day.

"I...that is, the Earl of Pembroke mistook me for a lady, and I did...that is, I did not exactly correct him."

When she had confessed all, Audrey was silent. Sean looked at her disapprovingly.

"Am I to be dismissed?" Gillian asked. It would not be uncalled for, given her outrageous behavior and deception.

"Dismissed?" Audrey tilted her head to one side, puzzled. "Why would I dismiss you?"

"Because I deceived Lord Pembroke and acted above my station."

Again, her mistress gazed at her, her head still tilted at a slight angle, her brown eyes bright.

"Perhaps someone else would dismiss you, but we aren't simply lady and lady's maid, Gillian. We are *friends*. I know you almost as well as you know yourself. I don't believe you were acting poorly with Lord Pembroke. He made an assumption, and you did not correct him. That is a matter we can worry about later. What is important is that you were unharmed. I wish for you to rest tonight. Sean will watch over you."

"And you will stay here, my lady? Stay safe?" Gillian pressed.

"I will stay safe," Audrey assured her. "Now let's get you into bed so you can rest."

Gillian left Audrey's study and climbed the flight of stairs to her private bedroom. Sean brought her another cup of tea and a bowl of soup, which smelled divine. After she'd eaten, she lay down on her narrow bed, pulled her quilt around her body, and closed her eyes. So much had happened today—things that had been frightening and things that had been wonderful.

She knew what she had done concerning James was wrong. She was not a lady like Audrey. But for just a few hours she'd forgotten how tired and anxious she was and how stifling her life as a maid could be. She was simply herself, Gillian, and she had kissed a wonderful and attractive nobleman.

She replayed their heated moment in the bookshop, burning it into her memory. It would keep her warm in the long, lonely nights to come. Gillian would never be a lady like her mistress, but she could let herself imagine what might have been were she Lord Pembroke's lady. A tear fell from her closed eyes, dampening her pillow.

I am a wicked maid for thinking such thoughts, but I wish I could be his wicked maid.

Thank you so much for reading this short story about Gillian and James! Be sure to sign up for my newsletter at www.laurensmithbooks.com so don't miss their full story which comes out March 13th, 2018 - The Earl of Pembroke- as part of the Wicked Earl's Club.

Get The Earl of Pembroke HERE!
Turn the page to see the cover and to start reading Audrey and Jonathan's Story!

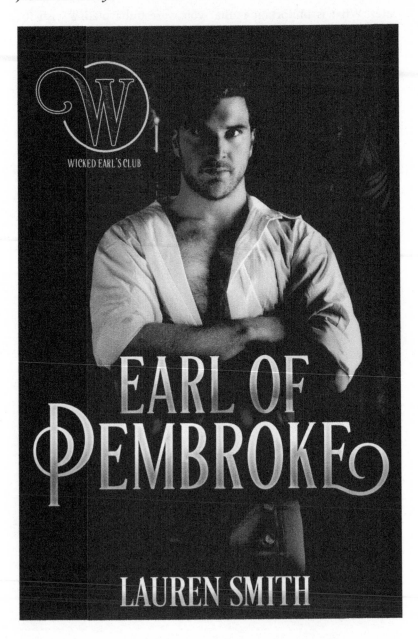

HIS WICKED LESSONS

A SHORT STORY

CHAPTER 1

A udrey Sheridan's eyes might have been on her reflection in her vanity mirror, but her mind was focused inward. Tonight, she was to embark on a dangerous mission: infiltrating a hellfire club in order to expose the members and their sordid acts to London society.

As the secret columnist Lady Society, she prided herself on the articles she wrote for *The Quizzing Glass Gazette*. She did not write silly little pieces of fluff on who was marrying whom or who had worn the latest fashions from Paris well—though she did so love to talk about fashion. Her articles were designed to push the boundaries of society.

After all, the *ton*, if left to itself, would remain complacent and unmoved. A stagnant ground bereft of new ideas and enshrining only old ones. A place where progress would not be tolerated, let alone embraced.

A smile curved her lips as she relished the thought of how tonight's foray into a dangerous club would shock everyone. She would be incognito, of course, but still, once she wrote the article exposing the gentlemen who belonged to the hellfire club, all of London would be shocked by the idea of the mysterious Lady

Society being in such danger and surviving with her identity still shrouded in mystery.

The problem was keeping her older brother, Cedric, and his friends, the League of Rogues, from discovering her plans. They were all such dears, but Lord, they could be so overprotective of her. She might as well have five older brothers rather than just one. Ever since their parents had died when she was a child, Cedric had become more than a brother—he'd transformed into a fierce guardian. He would've wrapped her in a giant ball of muslin to protect her if he could.

"There you are, my lady." Her lady's maid, Gillian Beaumont, tucked one delicate curl into place in Audrey's coiffure.

Audrey gazed at her maid in the mirror, wanting to see if the young woman would smile back. Gillian was so serious all the time. She and Audrey were both nineteen, but Gillian seemed so forlorn at times, as though she had lived many lifetimes before this, and none had ended well. It was Audrey who insisted on involving her maid in her wild schemes. She wanted her friend to live a little.

"Perfect. I have to look my best today. The League is coming over for tea in an hour and…" Audrey's cheeks heated as she could no longer push away the thought of the man who would soon be under her roof. She knew Gillian would assume she was going to stay here while they came for tea, but that was the last thing Audrey wanted. It had become painfully obvious that Jonathan St. Laurent did not want anything to do with her. He'd made his intentions perfectly clear last Christmas when he'd all but fled the room once she had attempted to seduce him.

He wants nothing to do with me, so I won't stay here and be polite.

Her feelings were bruised. More than bruised. She'd fallen in love with Jonathan soon after she'd met him and had dreamed of no other man since. Although her feelings toward him hadn't changed, she had her pride and was tired of trying to woo him.

"And Mr. St. Laurent will be there?" her maid asked.

"Err... I suppose so," she hedged. She really didn't want to speak of Jonathan anymore. "Gillian, could you run a few errands for me today? I believe we have a few articles to post in the *Quizzing Glass Gazette* that will need to run in the next few weeks. Would you mind seeing to that for me?"

She pulled the bodice of her gown up a little. The blue cambric muslin was a sensible choice, but the flare of the lavender gauze on the hem made her feel like a fairy queen. Everyone poked fun at her love of fashion, but none of them understood it was part of her power, with far greater range than any suspected. She could disguise herself as a lad or dress the part of a queen to great effect. She tilted her head as she realized Gillian hadn't answered her. Her maid was staring into the distance, her hands absently playing with a bit of her own gown.

"Well? Do you mind very much?"

Gillian's eyes widened and she focused on Audrey. "Of course, my apologies, my lady. I was woolgathering. Yes, leave me the articles, and I will see them placed in the proper hands."

"Excellent." Audrey walked to her escritoire, withdrew three articles she had carefully packaged, and handed them to Gillian.

"Do you need anything else, my lady?" Gillian asked.

"Not at the moment. Oh, and remember, tonight we will be going to that hellfire club."

Her maid stiffened, and the paper she held crinkled. "My lady, I really don't think we should—"

Audrey tapped her foot and crossed her arms. "Gillian, you know that awful Gerald Langley belongs to that club. What was it called?" She searched her memory. "Sinners and Sadists, no... Wait!" She lifted a finger in the air. "The Unholy Sinners of Hell."

Gillian openly flinched. "Must we go tonight? The men could be dangerous."

Dangerous? Lord, she hoped so. Life could be so tedious as a gently-bred lady. She craved the same freedom as men did to run about doing whatever they pleased.

"Nonsense. We should be perfectly fine. They allow ladies to attend their unholy festivities, and if we bring along Charles and his valet as escorts, we shall be quite safe."

Gillian stared at her. "Lord Lonsdale? He's not exactly a man of sterling reputation. You remember the swans. Everyone was so scandalized."

Audrey couldn't resist giggling. The swans. Everyone loved the swan story. "Of course I do. I was there. Charles isn't so bad. I had a bloody hard time trying to kiss him, you remember. He's more of a gentleman than he lets on."

Her maid gave a little huff and walked toward the door, but Audrey suddenly remembered one more thing she needed Gillian to do, which would keep her safely occupied while Audrey ran off this afternoon to pursue her training as a spy. She knew Gillian would disapprove, but Audrey had to do something, had to have some adventures.

"The dresses! I completely forgot. You must go to Madame Ella's and retrieve the gowns. Try them on to make sure they fit," Audrey said. She trusted the dressmaker's skill, but sometimes she wanted to give Gillian a taste of the life the other woman would never have the chance to experience. She was the daughter of an earl and would have been above Audrey under different circumstances, yet she had been forced into domestic service to keep her mother in decent living conditions. But Gillian was all alone now, except for Audrey, and she would not let Gillian fade away. Women needed to help one another.

Gillian sighed, her shoulders drooping as she nodded.

"Thank you." She escorted her maid to the door and gave her an encouraging little push. Audrey stood at the top of the stairs, watching her friend depart.

"Have fun today. You deserve it," she whispered, hoping that Gillian would use the day to be free of her role as a servant, just as Audrey would be free this afternoon of her own bondage as a highborn lady. When she was positive her watchful maid was gone, she returned to her room and checked her appearance once more, then removed the letter hidden in her dress pocket. She slipped out and read it again.

Miss Sheridan,

I will be happy to give you lessons in the arts of which we spoke, but you must be sure to come alone to the Midnight Garden. I cannot meet you at my residence. Be sure to arrive at half past one o'clock. Hire a coach and have it drop you off by the mews. A servant will be waiting to bring you inside.

Evangeline Mirabeau

Audrey carefully tore the letter into tiny pieces and tucked them into a drawer to dispose of later. She collected her reticule and checked the clock on the mantle. It was almost one o'clock now. She ought to leave before the League arrived for tea. If she had to explain why she was running off, her brother might suspect she was up to something... which she most certainly was.

As she exited her room again and started down the stairs, her sister-in-law Anne came out of the library, beaming at her.

"Audrey! I'm so glad I found you. Cedric and I would like to speak with you before everyone arrives."

Anne was positively glowing, and Audrey suspected the news her brother wanted to share involved a little Sheridan on the way. But she wouldn't spoil their moment of joy by letting them know she'd guessed. For the past week she'd watched her brother and Anne whisper to each other over breakfast and share secret smiles.

Audrey attempted to ignore a little prickle of envy. She wanted to be married to a man and love him the way Anne loved her brother. But Jonathan did not want her, and no other man had moved her the way he did. Therefore, she resolved to go it alone and become the proverbial spinster, but secretly live a life of spying and intrigue, assuming that Evangeline Mirabeau could help her learn the craft properly. Audrey knew she had to possess some skills to have uncovered society's secrets and go undetected as Lady Society for so long.

Anne slipped her arm through Audrey's, and they walked into her brother's study. Cedric was seated at his desk, the midday sun illuminating him as he read through a stack of letters.

"Cedric, I found Audrey." Anne flashed her warm smile, let go of Audrey's arm, and then walked over to her husband and kissed his cheek. Her brother grinned as he pushed his letters aside and stood. He curled one arm around Anne's waist, his brown eyes twinkling.

"Ah, good. I suppose Anne said we had news to share with you?"

"Yes." Audrey waited, letting them enjoy their news. She was so happy for them. Cedric had been blinded last Christmas and had all but lost his will to live. Marriage had saved him in more ways than one. His sight had returned and his spirits too. They both deserved great joy in their lives.

"We are expecting. It's still early yet, but we are quite hopeful."

Audrey's eyes filled with tears as she looked at her brother and his wife. They were both radiant with their love and the promise of their first child.

"Oh, Cedric, that is the most wonderful news!" She rushed over to him and embraced them both. Her brother let go of Anne to hug Audrey fiercely.

"I hope you don't mind being the doting aunt to our little one when the babe arrives?"

"Of course not!" She sniffed and wiped her eyes as he let go of her. Their other sister, Horatia, was also pregnant, but since she and Lucien lived in a separate townhouse, Audrey wouldn't see their child as much as this one under her own roof.

"But don't feel that you must stay," Anne said, her tone serious.

"All we want is for you to be happy, and it seems that lately..." Anne glanced at Cedric, sharing a worried look.

"That what?" Audrey asked.

"That you are lonely. I hate seeing you so Friday-faced, kitten." Cedric chucked her under her chin the way he had so often over the years. He had always looked out for her, always put her interests first. He'd been forced to grow up far too quickly and had become both father and mother to his sisters. Now he was ready to become a father to his own child, and she didn't wish to be a burden, but the truth was she couldn't live on her own. It wasn't done. Society thrust women into gilded cages, and they had no true independence.

"You used to be thrilled at the thought of balls and suitors. I promised to stop challenging your gentlemen callers, what has changed?" Cedric, as always, saw through her. But she didn't want to ruin his happy news by forcing her own concerns and sorrows on him.

She painted a bright smile upon her lips. "I'm fine."

"But—"

"I've been so melancholy of late because the fashions I like in gowns have changed. It can quite ruin a lady's happiness to change her wardrobe because of rising waistlines and fuller skirts." She giggled, though the sound rang false in her ears.

"Er...right." Cedric hesitated, his brotherly instincts warning him that something was amiss. She could see the suspicion in his eyes but hoped he wouldn't continue to press her.

A knock on the study door had them all turning to see a footman there.

"My lord, your afternoon guests have arrived," the lad said.

Cedric's worries evaporated as he faced Anne. "Ready to share the good news with the League?"

Anne nodded, a blush stealing upon her cheeks. "I can't wait. Three babes so close in age. It will be wonderful." Two others from the League were expecting children—which included Horatia and her husband Lucien.

"Indeed," Cedric agreed. Audrey stepped back to let them pass by her into the corridor. Her heart was beating rapidly. She knew who might be there.

Jonathan.

She didn't want to face him, not after the last time they'd been alone together. He'd dragged her away from Fives Court, where she'd been disguised as a boy to watch Charles in a boxing match. She'd been so confident then that her disguise had been good, but he'd seen right through her. He'd been furious she'd gone to such a place, especially disguised as a man. She had been exasperated with him and then furious when he'd dragged her away by her arm like a naughty child.

He'd taken her straight home in a coach, lecturing her the entire journey. She hadn't forgotten their argument. She had screamed at him that she wasn't a child, and he'd told her, *"I'll believe that when you start acting like the fine lady you're supposed to be."*

Fine lady. Jonathan didn't know the first thing about fine ladies. He had been raised as a servant, after all. The thought made her wince, not because he had once been a servant—she was not snobbish—but she knew he was sensitive on the matter. He'd only learned some months earlier that he was the legitimate son of the late Duke of Essex and the half brother of the current duke.

Jonathan had met a cloud of scandal when he was introduced into the *ton* last fall. The son of the lady's maid of the late duchess, born after a secret marriage and hidden in plain sight as valet to his own half brother...

None of that mattered to her, of course. She loved a good scandal. It was her forte, after all, as Lady Society.

The entryway exploded with noise as the entire League paraded through the front door. Audrey hung back, leaning against the doorjamb of Cedric's study as she saw Horatia and her husband Lucien, the Marquess of Rochester, enter first. Godric, the Duke of Essex, and his wife, Emily, came next, followed by Ashton, Baron Lennox and his wife, Rosalind. Charles, the Earl of Lonsdale, was absent, much to Audrey's concern.

She was worried about Charles. Each time one of the League of Rogues married, it left him more and more closed off. His remoteness was unnatural, yet she understood what he might be feeling. There was something sad about watching her family and friends marry and leave her behind. They didn't exclude her on purpose, but she felt alone all the same. Charles had to be experiencing similar feelings. It made sense.

"Audrey!" Horatia, as always, sought her out at once. The lovely rose-colored gown she wore was full at the waist as the curve of her unborn child showed. Horatia embraced her tightly, her brown eyes searching Audrey's.

"You look unwell. Why don't we go somewhere and talk?" Horatia suggested.

"No, I'm fine, quite fine, I assure you." She smiled and placed her palm on Horatia's belly. "How is my future niece or nephew today?"

Her sister beamed. "Lively. He's been kicking like a devil."

"He?" Audrey clung to that word.

Horatia chuckled. "I have dreams about the baby and it is always a he. Lucien swears it's a girl because of the trouble she makes when the baby kicks and wakes me up at night."

"I agree with you, it sounds more like a boy because he's causing trouble." Audrey smiled, feeling better as she imagined Horatia and Lucien's child and the mischief the little boy or girl might get into.

Before she could speak further, the entire League had moved toward the drawing room for tea. Audrey watched them go, but made no move to follow. Instead, she clutched her reticule and headed for the front door. She'd only just reached for the handle when the door opened. Stumbling back, she blinked against the bright light from the doorway and the tall figure silhouetted there.

"Oh... Miss Sheridan," Jonathan's voice was as smooth and rich as honey to her ears.

Damnation! She'd hoped to escape before he arrived.

"Mr. St. Laurent." She recovered quickly and stepped back, allowing him to enter. When he was out of the bright light and she was able to see him better, she saw he wore buckskin trousers that clung to his lean, muscled legs and a maroon waistcoat that made his sandy brown hair gleam. His green eyes always glinted devilishly, as though he knew secrets she'd give anything to know.

"Pardon me, I was just about to—"

"Flee?" he suggested, one dark gold brow raised.

Was he accusing her of running away? She inwardly cursed. He was right, she *was* fleeing him, but she didn't like to think he was able to read her so easily.

"I was not fleeing," she replied archly. "I have things to do and cannot have tea with everyone." She started to walk around him to leave, but he caught her arm, holding her captive.

"Aren't you forgetting something?" he asked, his voice still soft and husky, a tone more suited to a lover's whisper in the bedchamber. The air between them was thick with unspoken words and a tension that sent shivers through her as that forbidden desire rose up within her.

She glanced down at herself, then around. "No..."

He rolled his eyes. "A chaperone. You need one. Where's Gillian?" His hold on her arm tightened and her body hummed with hungers she'd vowed to ignore no matter how badly she wanted to indulge them. Anger flared inside her at his words. Yet again, he was chastising her like a child while he made her feel wild and hot...

She narrowed her eyes at him. "A chaperone? I most certainly do *not* need one, and Gillian is running errands for me. Now good day." She tugged her arm free and stalked in a rather unladylike fashion down the steps to the street, and waited for her hired hackney to come collect her.

Bloody rogue! I shouldn't have to be watched every instant.

She did not look back, not once, even when the hired cab stopped in front of her and she told the driver her destination as she climbed inside.

Foolish, odious man!

Audrey stared out the window and tried to focus on the lessons she was about to have. Her tutor was Evangeline Mirabeau, the former mistress of Jonathan's half- brother, Godric. That information had been surprisingly easy to obtain; the mistress of a duke tended to have a reputation, after all. What Audrey had been most interested in was not Evangeline's relationship with Godric, but rather how she'd come to England and made a life for herself.

Most ladies would be scandalized even speaking a courtesan's name, but Audrey was not most ladies. Evangeline was French, and she knew much about the trouble on the Continent. She had been forced to flee when her aristocratic family had been killed. She'd fought her way to England, only to become a courtesan in order to survive. Rather than judge her, Audrey respected her for her strength.

As the coach stopped in front of the Midnight Garden, Audrey shivered. She'd never been inside a house of ill repute before, but this was the best place to meet Evangeline. The patrons of the Garden would keep her identity a secret, just as she would keep their names private, since none would admit to being present. One might call it mutually-assured discretion.

The driver stopped at the entrance to the mews just between the Midnight Garden and the next townhouse. She exited the coach and paid the man to return in two hours. Audrey squared her shoulders and rushed down the narrow mews to a door which was opened by a man after just one knock. The servant was a handsome man with a ready smile that made Audrey's heart skip.

She had been warned before by Evangeline about the servants of the Garden and how seductive they could be.

"Welcome, my lady," the man purred. "Have you chosen your pleasure for this afternoon, or may I offer my services?" The man gestured for her to follow him into a sitting room down the hall. Everything in the room they entered was red. She blushed as she remembered that her sister had once sneaked in here to meet with Lucien. That particular rogue adored the color red. Was this where he had found his love of the color?

"I have an appointment with Miss Mirabeau." Audrey's body reacted as the man leaned down to where she sat on the couch and caressed the back of his knuckles over her cheek.

"A female? I am most disappointed. It has been ages since I've tasted a young, pretty peach like you."

"I'm afraid you'll have to wait a while longer." A dark growl came from the doorway behind the handsome servant.

Audrey gasped as she moved to the side, leaning past the man to see who had spoken. It was just as she feared.

She had been followed.

CHAPTER 2

Jonathan St. Laurent walked up the steps to the Sheridan townhouse, his heart racing. *She* was inside. The little sprite who had fueled too many fantasies of late. Her dark-brown eyes gazing into his, the deep rich coils of her russet-brown locks spread out over a pillow, her lips parted as she gasped and moaned his name. She was a woman full of passion—and she scared the bloody hell out of him. She was the only woman he'd ever met who seemed to know exactly who she was and what she wanted out of life. She'd never want a man like him, not really. Her interest in him was no more than a game to her.

And I'm the fool who wants to marry her, if she'll have me.

He paused at the closed door, hesitating. Sweat gathered in his palms as he fought off a rush of nerves. He tugged on his riding gloves, trying to prepare himself to enter. Jonathan paused as he stared hard at the iron lion's head knocker.

Last Christmas he had made a mess of things, but to be fair, she'd caught him off guard. Lucien had been fighting with Horatia, and he'd encouraged Jonathan to take a firm hold of Audrey and take her up to her room.

It hadn't gone well at all.

He'd lost control and carried the woman out of the room in his arms. She'd smacked him soundly with a rolled-up fashion-plate magazine and wriggled like a fish. By the time he got her upstairs, his temper and passions were so utterly mixed he couldn't separate them enough to clear his head. He'd tossed her onto the bed, and she had pulled him down on top of her.

That first kiss—Lord, she had tasted sweet. Her mouth had been as soft as petals and as hot as fire. He had lost control. She was a woman a man could kiss for days and never want to stop. He almost hadn't. Jonathan had given in to his desires, pinning her down on her bed and claiming her mouth in all the ways he'd dreamed about for months.

And then she'd done something no gentle-born young lady should have known how to do. She'd *stroked* him. Her touch on his cock, even through his trousers, had nearly killed him. He'd rolled off her and fled the room. If he'd stayed, he would have taken her, with little if any ability to restrain himself.

I've been running ever since.

He wanted her so much it hurt, but she was too good for him. Even though her brother and the rest of the League had encouraged the match, Jonathan still felt unworthy. He'd been raised as a servant until he'd turned twenty-four. And then his well-organized world had been turned on its head when he learned he was not only Godric's half brother, but a *legitimate* son of their father.

The truth of his birth, although well known, was still spoken of in whispers. Audrey didn't deserve that kind of cloud over her social life, and he knew how much balls and parties mattered to her. She was a woman who enjoyed life, a woman who loved to laugh, smile, and dance. Until London stopped whispering about him, he couldn't take a chance by asking her to marry him, no matter how much he wished to.

Having stared at the knocker long enough, he decided against using it and simply entered the townhouse, expecting to find the

League filling the hall. Instead, he found himself colliding with the very woman who vexed him.

"Oh… Miss Sheridan," he managed to say, startled by her loveliness. She blinked and squinted at him, but he didn't care. She looked as lovely as a woman dressed for a ball. Hell, she'd even looked lovely masquerading as a boy at Fives Court and shouting curses like any man at a boxing match.

Lord, he found her a fascinating creature.

"Mr. St. Laurent," she replied, her tone frosty. That was certainly his fault. The last time they'd been alone, he'd dragged her away from Fives Court and lectured her on the dangers. She had no idea how precarious her position had been. Fives Court drew gentlemen, but also the dregs of society, men who wouldn't have backed down had they discovered she was a woman. When he'd realized it was her and not one of the boys worshiping at the altar of Charles as he boxed, Jonathan's heart had almost leapt out of his chest. His only thought had been to get her to safety. And that little hellion was holding it against him.

Audrey tried to get around him. "Pardon me, I was just about to—"

"Flee?" He arched an eyebrow. She was running away, something she didn't usually do. Her face was pale and her eyes a little red. She'd been upset? He did the only thing he could do. He challenged her to stay and argue with him.

"I was *not* fleeing," she snapped, lifting her chin defiantly. "I have things to do. I cannot have tea with everyone."

Jonathan grasped her arm, holding her still. He could feel the heat of her skin against his, which set fire to his blood. The urge to swing her around to face him and kiss her was almost overpowering. The only thing that stopped him was knowing her brother was but one door away, and while Cedric approved of the match, he would not approve of his sister being kissed like a common wench in view of everyone. That would get him shot in an instant, even if the kiss was worth dying for.

He tried to bury the thought of kissing her and focus on the fact that she was leaving the house alone.

"Aren't you forgetting something?"

The look of confusion as she glanced around would have made him laugh on any other occasion. She was so confident she didn't even think about chaperones. Stubborn creature... adorably stubborn.

"No." She glowered at him and he rolled his eyes.

"A chaperone. You need one. Where's Gillian?" He searched the hall for Audrey's maid. Being a former servant, he never took them for granted. Audrey's maid was usually quite good at keeping her mistress out of trouble. Gillian was normally Audrey's shadow. The two were rarely apart, but there was no sign of the quiet lady's maid now.

"A chaperone? I certainly do *not* need one, and Gillian is running errands for me. Now good day." She ripped her arm from his with surprising force for one so small. He wanted to stop her, to call out and beg her to stay, but he was frozen at the top of the steps as she hurried away into a hired coach. Where the devil was she off to?

"Sir, would you like to join the others for tea?" the footman, Sean Hartley, asked. Jonathan spun to face him.

"Er... No. Do you know where Miss Sheridan went?"

Sean shook his head. "I wish I knew. She made no mention to the staff that she was leaving."

"Hellfire and damnation!" Jonathan cursed. "Sean, fetch my horse." He ran back to the steps, keeping his eye on Audrey's coach as it rattled down the street. A minute later, a groom returned with his horse, which hadn't been settled within the Sheridan stables. Jonathan merely nodded at the groom before he swung himself up into the saddle and dug his heels into the horse's flanks. He urged it into a canter to catch up with Audrey's coach, but not too close. He couldn't let her know he was following her, at least not until he figured out what she was up to.

Her coach stopped in front of an establishment he knew only too well. The Midnight Garden. It was a high-end brothel, but still a damned brothel and no place for virginal gently-born ladies like Audrey. Jonathan reined his horse in, slowing enough that he stayed far back from her hackney. Should she decide to glance around, he didn't want her to see him.

"What the devil are you up to?" he muttered as he dismounted and walked his horse toward the entrance of the Garden. He could see Audrey disappear into a door at the side of the building. A servant came down the steps to take his horse, and Jonathan handed the mare over to him.

"Where does that door lead?" he asked the man as he pointed at the side entrance.

"Private rooms for gentlemen or ladies who have made appointments and don't wish to be seen."

Jonathan huffed. So, Audrey thought she could go to a house of pleasure to satisfy her urges? Over his dead body. He'd known the moment he'd kissed her at Christmas that she was no wilting flower or trembling virgin who feared passion. She was a wanton, wild creature who longed for physical love as much as he did, but if she wanted someone to experience lovemaking with, it would not be some man in a pleasure den. Audrey deserved to learn at the hands of a gentleman, or at least someone who was doing his best to be one at the moment.

He strode down the alley, ignoring the shout from the servant to stop. If the man came after him, he would lay the fellow flat with one good punch.

When he reached the door, he found it unlocked. He burst inside, not knowing what to expect, and was surprised to find a silk-wallpapered corridor with gilded lamps that resembled the rest of the house. There were doors along either side, which probably contained entertaining rooms. Most of the bedrooms were upstairs.

"My lord?" a woman asked as she exited a chamber next to

him. Her partially exposed bosom and painted face were meant to enhance her looks, but they failed.

"I'm looking for a woman, this high." He held his hand up to his chest, showing the other woman how short Audrey was. "She's wearing a blue cambric gown and has dark hair and dark eyes."

"She's with Rufus, the first door on the left," the woman whispered huskily. He ignored her open invitation.

He stomped past her. "Thank you." When he reached the door, it was partially open. The voices were soft murmurs, but he knew if he opened the door, he'd hear better. Jonathan braced himself for a fight as he nudged the door with his boot hard enough that it swung open. He saw a tall man leaning over a couch, and Audrey's slippered feet were visible between the man's parted thighs. The man had cornered her against the couch. His words filled Jonathan with a blinding rage.

"It has been ages since I've tasted a young, pretty peach like you."

Curling his hands into fists, Jonathan took one step into the room.

"I'm afraid you'll have to wait a while longer."

The man, Rufus, spun, his eyes widening. "My lord?" He stepped sideways, avoiding blocking Audrey from Jonathan's view. *Smart man.* If Rufus had tried to stay between him and Audrey, Jonathan would have laid him out with one good punch.

"The lady does not require your services," Jonathan informed him. "So get the bloody hell out of this room before I throw you out."

Rufus shot one last glance at Audrey before he bolted.

"Mr. St. Laurent!" Audrey leapt up from the couch, a honeyed fire lighting her brown eyes as she came toe to toe with him. "How *dare* you follow me. How *dare* you interrupt my private engagement!"

"Private engagement? You are not going to be needing any *services* here. Do you understand?"

Audrey raised her reticule and whacked him soundly on the shoulder.

"Oomph!" He winced. What did she have inside the damned glittery little bag?

"Get out of my way. I'm going to find the madam and have you thrown out." She started to march past him like a feisty army general, but he caught her by the waist. Before she could stop him, he tossed her over his shoulder and left the room. If she wanted lessons in seduction, she was going to be schooled by him and no one else.

CHAPTER 3

Audrey's breath burst from her lungs as Jonathan climbed the central stairs leading up to the other rooms in the Midnight Garden. He stopped only once, to demand a bedchamber, while Audrey shrieked until he smacked her arse with one hand. The blow hadn't hurt, but the message it sent was clear—she was no longer in charge. Normally, a loss of control would terrify her, but with Jonathan, it heated her blood. It made her feel faint.

Probably because you're hanging upside down, you silly fool. She refused to let her body betray her, not when she had vowed to stop finding Jonathan attractive.

He opened the door to the bedroom and slid the lock into place with a frightening finality before he set her down on the bed. Audrey's breath came easier. She would recover from being carried around like a sack of potatoes. Her artfully styled hair had started to come undone, and she pulled a few pins out of her messy locks and tossed them to the floor in frustration.

"Why didn't you just take me home?" she demanded, refusing to look at him as she peered at her reflection in the full-length mirror across the room. Her hair was not salvageable.

Jonathan laughed harshly. "First, tell me *exactly* why you are here. Do you have any idea how furious your brother would be if he found you at a brothel?"

She shrugged. "He has much more on his mind now than me. He and Anne are expecting. He doesn't have time to worry about me anymore, and you shouldn't either. No one appointed you my guardian, so stop playing the part. He already likes you, all of them do, so you need not protect me to be in their good graces." She slid off the bed and approached the mirror.

Her body flushed with heat as he stepped up behind her. He was so tall compared to her. When she met his gaze in the mirror, she saw the infamous St. Laurent temper lurking there. It was not the sort of temper that made one fear for one's safety. When he was angry, like his older brother, he expelled his fury through sensual domination. Like kissing her to silence her protestations.

Audrey truly feared this—not because she didn't want him to dominate her like that, but because she would like it far too much, and it would rob her of her good sense.

"Audrey." The roughness of his usually silky voice made her tremble. She raised her chin defiantly.

"Take me home. I don't care." But she did. He might have already ruined her plans to meet with Evangeline.

"You do care," Jonathan said, his tone softening. "You have hungers and desires like a man, and it must be very frustrating to have no one to learn from." His green eyes were piercing, seeing right through her bravado. How could he know that was exactly how she felt? Trapped by her own desires, with no way to learn how to enjoy herself because of the restrictions society put on women when it came to passion? Her future husband would've shown her, but she couldn't marry just anyone. She wanted a love match and had hoped that *this man* would want her. But he didn't.

"No other man will teach you." The fierce determination in his eyes made her want to scream in frustration.

"Just because you do not want me, that doesn't mean you can simply lock me away in a tower to die a spinster!" She started to turn around, fully intending to smack him, but he suddenly moved. He slid one arm around her waist, holding her captive and pressing her back to his chest. His other hand gripped her throat, not hard, but the possessive hold sent a riotous shiver of dark longing through her. His palm rubbed gently along her neck as he pressed his lips to the shell of her ear.

"I never once said I didn't want you. I want you too much... that's exactly the problem. That servant was right. You are sweet as a peach, and I've dreamt of a thousand ways I would take you." The devilish whisper in her ear made her blood pound so hard it felt like a dull roar.

"You...want me?" Surely, he was teasing her, toying with her to some cruel end. If he wanted her, he wouldn't have abandoned her or resisted her when she tried to show him her desire.

"So badly that it makes my body ache. Do you know what it feels like?" Jonathan growled. His hand at her waist slid down her skirts along her thigh. He began to drag her gown up. Audrey gasped as his palm touched her stocking-clad knee.

"What does it feel like?" Her question escaped her lips in a ragged whisper.

Jonathan nibbled the lobe of her ear. Tiny sparks shot down to her abdomen. A heavy heat filled her deep inside, and a pulsing started between her thighs.

"It feels like I'll die if I don't taste you, if I don't pin you down on the bed and ravish you. Every muscle in my body is rigid with *need*." He rocked his hips against hers, and she felt the bulge of his arousal dig into her lower back. The pulsing inside her grew harder, and she panted softly. His hand underneath her skirts had reached the middle of her thighs, and he now drew teasing patterns on the bare skin of her leg. Audrey couldn't speak—she was captivated by his words and how he made her feel.

"I've often wondered if you were some kind of witch, the way you cast a spell over me. I can't get to sleep at night without picturing myself claiming you over and over." His dark-gold lashes fell halfway as he flicked his tongue inside her ear. Audrey whimpered at the burst of arousing new sensations elicited by the naughty little lick of his tongue. Unable to stop, she pressed her hips back, rubbing herself against him. It was a completely wanton thing to do, but she didn't care. She needed him to deliver the passion his hands and mouth were promising.

"Please, Jonathan, stop torturing me!" she begged.

His raspy chuckle gave her delicious chills. "Torturing you? Oh, my darling. I haven't even begun." His hand between her legs moved higher, slowly, deliberately teasing until he reached her aching sex. When he cupped her mound, she arched her back as a flood of sensations exploded through her. She felt dizzy, and her legs shook as he played with her. There was no other word but *play* to describe the featherlight touches on her bundle of nerves and the little strokes along her inner folds, which were slick with her arousal.

"Already wet for me." He purred the words in a low rumble that she felt vibrate from his chest to her back.

She couldn't think past the fact that Jonathan had his fingers inside her, was caressing her in the most secret part of her body, and then...

The climax hit her hard, so hard she cried out, but he held on to her, like a hound with a kitten in its paws. She stared at their reflection, seeing his wolfish smile as he pressed a kiss to her cheek and murmured soft words of nonsense in her ear. Her heart was racing, and her body shook violently. She felt as though she'd almost died in that instant before she'd seemed to explode from the inside out.

"I...don't think I can walk," she whispered. Her legs were locked in place, and her body quivered as he slowly withdrew his hand from between her legs and let her dress fall back into place.

"Hold on, my darling." He lifted her up in his arms and cradled her to his chest as he carried her to the bed. He set her down and then joined her, leaning back against the pillows as he cuddled her to him.

Audrey felt *raw*...exposed in a way that made no sense. She rarely felt shy or vulnerable, but she did now.

I've never really thought this through. Kissing a rogue is one thing, but making love...

It was too much, the sensations too frightening. And she hadn't even done the deed completely.

"What's the matter?" Jonathan's green eyes darkened with worry.

"I should go," she gasped, scrambling from the bed. Her reticule lay abandoned on the floor. She snatched it up.

"Audrey, stop and rest. After an experience like that, you need to have a few minutes to recover."

Recover? She almost laughed. She would never recover from what they'd just done.

"No, I must leave. I'm missing tea..." she murmured, hating how foolish the words sounded. She tried to pull the door open, but couldn't.

"You're not missing tea." Jonathan was there behind her, one hand braced against the door, using his weight and strength to keep it shut.

"Please," she whispered. "*Please.*" She wasn't sure what she was asking. He settled a hand on her waist and gently pulled her back against him, holding her close. The tender embrace made her want to cry, but she didn't know why.

"That was your first time, wasn't it?" he asked, pressing a kiss to the crown of her hair. She nodded mutely.

"The French call it 'the little death' because it can be frightening at first, but then wonderful."

He was right. It had been frightening and then wonderful, but that wasn't what she feared. What she feared was the aftermath, the potent longing that seemed to cling to her heart when she thought of him holding her, kissing her, and making her feel such wondrous things. Here, in the Midnight Garden, he no doubt saw her presence as an open invitation, one without commitment or consequence. Audrey didn't want a broken heart. She refused to let a man be in control of her feelings. Love had seemed to be such a grand adventure, but now she didn't want to play the game and risk not being loved in return.

"Come back to bed with me." Jonathan pressed his lips to her neck, and she shivered in his hold.

"Horatia will be missing me," she tried to argue.

"Then let her." Jonathan turned her around in his arms and lifted her chin so her eyes met his. The soft expression there threatened to kill her with its sweetness. He lowered his head to hers and kissed her. Such a gentle kiss, his mouth moving over hers in a way that filled her body with a slow wave of heat. She finally understood how a woman could swoon in a man's arms. Kissing Jonathan made her feel light-headed, like she'd had too much sherry to drink. When their mouths parted, he rubbed the pads of his thumb over her cheeks.

"Feeling better?"

"Yes," she whispered.

"Good, because I need to speak with you. About *us*." His green eyes were like summer glens, dark emerald and full of secrets.

Speak about us? There is no us. He doesn't want there to ever be an us. She pulled free of him. Anything he wanted to say would crush her.

"No. Whatever you want to say, don't. I won't agree, and I don't want to hear it." She pulled the door open and fled into the corridor.

"Audrey, wait!" Jonathan called her name, but she didn't stop. She would never stop running away from the man who would break her heart.

∾

Jonathan swallowed down the acidic taste of disappointment as he watched Audrey flee. The words *"Will you marry me?"* withered upon his lips and died. She didn't even want to hear him out. He'd given up on resisting her and had decided he would take the risk and propose.

But now she didn't want him. Had it all been some elaborate game she was playing? Seduce a former servant and risk the scandal? When faced with actually marrying him, she ran away as fast as she could.

Jonathan leaned back against the wall in the bedchamber, his chest tight with an almost unbearable pain. He didn't want any other woman, *could* have no other but the very woman who didn't want him.

He glanced at the mirror, replaying every exquisite and

torturous moment of having Audrey come apart in his arms. He'd received no pleasure of his own other than watching her climax. She'd closed her eyes, those dark sooted lashes fanned across her cheeks and those kissable lips parted, her pink kittenish tongue licking them as she panted. Lord, she had tempted him like no other.

"Well, if it isn't Monsieur St. Laurent." A cool feminine chuckle came from the doorway. He turned to see Evangeline Mirabeau watching him. She was a lovely woman, all her curves displayed in a thin, dampened gown. Her honey-blonde hair hung in perfect ringlets. She was a true French courtesan.

"Miss Mirabeau," he greeted.

She smiled, a knowing smile. "Once, long ago, you and I were more intimate than that."

He didn't want that reminder. She'd been a fine lover, and her beauty was unquestionable, but the passions she had once roused in him were a mere candle flame compared to the inferno that Audrey created inside him.

"Yes," he agreed. "Once, but no longer."

"You wound me with such certainty. Ah well, *c'est la vie*." Evangeline glanced around the room. "Well, where's your petite friend? The Sheridan girl? I assume you escorted her here for her lessons?"

"Lessons?" He raised a brow at the woman, completely confused. Audrey came here to learn how to be a courtesan?

The Frenchwoman tilted her head. The amusement in her eyes dimmed as she grew serious. "You do not know?"

"Know what?"

"That she is interested in...foreign etiquette?"

Jonathan shifted restlessly as he tried to understand what Evangeline was saying. "Etiquette...I don't... What does that have to do with you?"

"Ah, I see. You care for her, *n'est-ce pas*? You came here out of concern for her safety?" She sighed, as if she was about to do

75

something she was not accustomed to doing. "I do not expose a client's secrets, but if you do care for her so, then I suppose you should know. Her intention to learn the ways of the French court are not simply for fancy balls."

"What do you mean?"

"I cannot say, but perhaps your friend Avery Russell would."

"Avery?" Suddenly, Evangeline's mysterious comments made sense. "She's here to learn how to be a spy?" Jonathan sputtered out the word. "Audrey wasn't here to learn the art of seduction?"

"*Mais non,* we covered that over tea a few months ago."

What the devil did she need to learn how to spy for?

And then it hit him. She spent a lot of time with Charles, and Charles from time to time assisted Lucien Russell's younger brother, Avery, with his espionage missions within London. Audrey had been practicing disguises, but he hadn't realized that she would actually seek someone out to teach her how to be a spy.

Evangeline was still smiling. "I'll have to reschedule with her since you scared her off." The woman looked at him expectantly and didn't seem to care that she actually *had* exposed her client's secret.

With a low growl, he fished out a few pound notes and handed them to her.

"That's for today, and this"—he added a few more banknotes —"is to refuse to help her next time. She's too innocent for spy work. I don't want her in danger."

"*Mon ami,* unless you intend to lock *la petite femme* away, I think we both know she will do just as she pleases."

Jonathan groaned at this. Evangeline was right.

"And," she continued, "if that is the case, it is better to be prepared than not, *oui?* Which course of action truly puts her in more danger?"

"Fine. If she comes to you again for anything, and I mean *anything,* you write to me at once. I want to be involved."

He waited for Evangeline to nod before he let go of the last note he'd been holding out to her. Then he stormed out of the chamber. Today had been an awful mess. Not only had the woman he cared about told him she would never consider his proposal, he'd learned she was risking her life to play out fantasies of spies and intrigue. Jonathan knew he would have to tell her siblings; they would have to make her see reason.

I cannot be her husband, but I will still do everything in my power to protect her.

~

By the time Audrey entered the Sheridan house, she was in a daze, her emotions running rampant. She knew she looked a fright, her hair unbound, her dress wrinkled, but she couldn't help it. All she could do was get upstairs and collect herself.

"My lady!" Gillian gasped as she and Sean the footman hurried toward her from the servants' stairs.

"Gillian?" Audrey stared at the maid. The other woman looked as poorly as she did.

"Yes, my lady."

Sean stepped forward. "My lady, we must speak with you. I'm afraid it's a matter of urgency."

"Oh?" Audrey started for the stairs. She had her own private study, and it would be a good place to speak. Sean was the only person besides Gillian she trusted with her identity as Lady Society, and this would be far from their first secret meeting. It was a good thing her brother and the League were likely still having tea. She shut the door once Gillian and Sean were inside, and then she sat down at her desk.

"My lady, you received a warning from Mr. Worthing. You must not go through with tonight's plan," Gillian pleaded.

Worthing was warning her away from the hellfire club?

"But why not? You know those men are monsters. I cannot let them continue their awful meetings." She did not say that part of her was so upset she felt reckless enough to not heed their warnings.

"My lady, there was a man. He attacked me to get that letter given to me by Mr. Worthing."

"Attacked? Heavens, Gillian, are you all right?" Audrey leapt to her feet and went straight to her maid and firmly sat her down in the chair. "Please, sit. I had no idea." Gillian attacked... Audrey swallowed down a wave of guilt. She had brought her maid to this danger, and it was all her fault.

"I'm all right. Lord Pembroke assisted me and escorted me home."

James Fordyce had helped Gillian?

"He did? James is such a dear," she murmured. She had always adored him. He was a handsome man and very caring. It seemed he was always on the verge of rescuing ladies, even though they didn't usually need help.

"I should thank him," she added.

"No!" Gillian said. "I...that is, the Earl of Pembroke mistook me for a lady, and I did...that is, I did not exactly correct him."

This caught Audrey by surprise. Her quiet, no-rule-breaking maid had pretended to be a lady? Rather than be furious, Audrey was impressed.

"Am I to be dismissed?" It was hard to miss the sorrow in Gillian's tone.

"Dismissed?" Audrey tilted her head. "Why would I dismiss you?"

"Because I deceived Lord Pembroke and acted above my station."

"Perhaps someone else would dismiss you, but we aren't simply lady and lady's maid, Gillian. We are *friends*. I know you almost as well as you know yourself. I don't believe you were acting poorly with Lord Pembroke. He made an assumption, and you did not correct it. That is a matter we can worry about later. What is important is that you were unharmed. I wish for you to rest tonight. Sean will watch over you."

"And you will stay here, my lady? Stay safe?" Gillian pressed.

The earnestness that the maid showed in asking this made the guilt rise all over again, because Audrey was going to lie to her, the one friend she trusted like a sister.

"I will stay safe," she assured Gillian. "Now let's get you into bed so you can rest."

Sean escorted Gillian from Audrey's study. When they were gone, she collapsed into a chair, tucking her knees up to her chin. She didn't want to think about everything that had happened today. Her encounter with Jonathan left her feeling hollow and heartbroken. She had never been this weak before. She hated the very word. Her brother and sister, while protective of her, had never let her cultivate a weak personality.

I will not let a man break my heart and crush me. I will not.

She had to deceive Gillian tonight. She was going to expose Gerald Langley and his friends for the wretched men they were. It would undoubtedly be dangerous, but she'd already done the most dangerous thing she could, in her opinion, when she'd let herself go in Jonathan's arms.

His wicked lessons had proved she had so much to learn, and yet she would never have the chance, not with this man who didn't truly want her. Audrey brushed away her tears and went in search of another maid to help her prepare for tonight. She would go alone, broken heart be damned.

Thank you so much for reading this short story about Audrey and Jonathan! Be sure to sign up for my newsletter at www. laurensmithbooks.com so you don't miss their full story which comes out in 2018 - His Wicked Secret. Turn the page to see the cover! (Also keep reading to see a 3 chapter sneak peek of a new upcoming League of Rogues story)

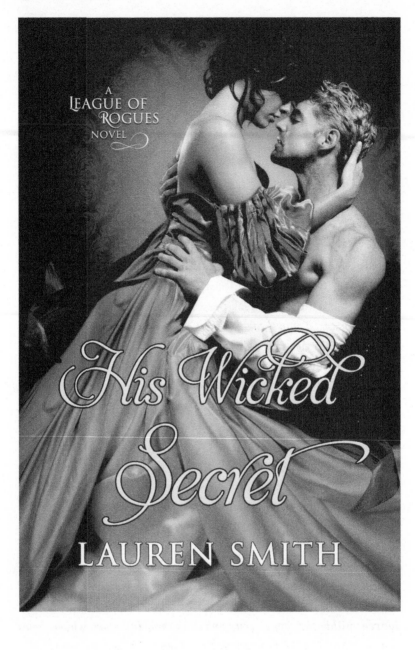

A LEAGUE OF ROGUES NOVEL

His Wicked Secret

LAUREN SMITH

Want three free romance novels? Fill out the form at the bottom of this link and you'll get an email from me with details to collect your free read! The free books are Wicked Designs (Historical romance), Legally Charming (contemporary romance) and The Bite of Winter (paranormal romance)

Claim your free book now at: http://laurensmithbooks.com/free-books-and-newsletter/, follow me on twitter at @LSmithAuthor, or like my Facebook page at https://www.facebook.com/LaurenDianaSmith. I share upcoming book news, snippets and cover reveals plus PRIZES!

Reviews help other readers find books. I appreciate all reviews, whether positive or negative. If one of my books spoke to you, please share!

You've just read the 5th book in the League of Rogues series. The other books in the series are *Wicked Designs, His Wicked Seduction, Her Wicked Proposal,* and *Wicked Rivals.* I hope you enjoy them all! There are more League adventures on the way! The sixth book *His Wicked Embrace* (which is about Lawrence Russell and Zehra Darzi) comes out in a box set this November called The Scoundrel Who Loved Me and as a individual book in March 5th 2018!

Want to read the first chapter of any of my books to see if you like it? Check out my Wattpad.com page where I post the first chapter of every book including ones not yet released! To start reading visit: https://www.wattpad.com/user/LaurenSmithAuthor.

If you'd like to read the first three chapters from *His Wicked Embrace*, the 6th book in this series, please turn the page.

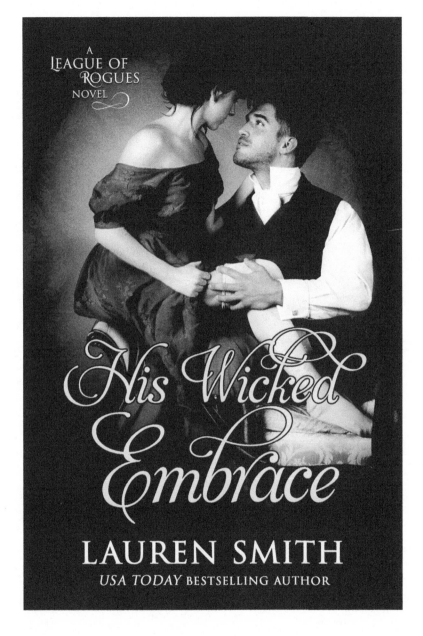

A LEAGUE OF ROGUES NOVEL

His Wicked Embrace

LAUREN SMITH

USA TODAY BESTSELLING AUTHOR

HIS WICKED EMBRACE

CHAPTER 1

L eague Rule Number 11:
    A man should remember from time to time to be a
gentleman, even if he thinks he may have forgotten how.

Excerpt from the *Quizzing Glass Gazette*, April 28, 1821, the Lady
Society column:

Lady Society is quite curious about a certain gentleman named Mr.
Lawrence Russell. His elder brother, the Marquess of Rochester, is quite
infamous indeed as a member of the League of Rogues, but as for Mr.
Russell himself...the rumors abound.

   Lady Society would like very much to know if he wishes to be
married, or will he continue as his brother had and resist matrimony at
all odds? If it is the former, Lady Society will endeavor to find him a
suitable bride; if it is the latter, Lady Society sees his determined bache-
lordom as a challenge. A rogue you may be, Mr. Russell, but Lady
Society believes you might yet make a good husband. Now who to marry
you to?

. . .

"You belong to me now."

The whispered words echoed in Zehra Darzi's head as she jolted awake. Somehow in the last twenty-four hours she'd managed to sleep a little inside her gilded prison. Those words that haunted her still made her head throb as a fresh wave of fear swept through her. The man who had spoken them had murdered her parents and kidnapped her from her palace in Persia three weeks ago.

Al-Zahrani. His name was like bitter poison upon her tongue, and she fought the urge to throw up. She'd spent only a few days as his prisoner—listening to him boast of capturing her and his plans of using her as a concubine—before she'd had a chance to flee.

She curled her hands into fists and winced as her nails dug into her palms. Cuts, somewhat healed, still stung from when she'd scaled a low-branched tree near Al-Zahrani's walls to break free. She'd been so close to freedom, had felt it with every step as she stumbled and ran through the desert hills.

Then, after two days without food or water, she'd collapsed on the dunes, lips parched and cracked, eyes burning. She'd glimpsed men upon the horizon, on horseback in dark clothes. At first she'd thought they were her salvation, but she soon learned they were anything but.

Slavers.

Now she was imprisoned in an English brothel thousands of miles from her home.

Zehra's gaze darted around the room for the hundredth time, and she wished the women who had seen to her care, such as it was, had brought a fresh pitcher of water. Her throat was parched and she would have done almost anything for a sip of water. It was dark outside, and she hadn't been visited by anyone since early that morning, when the slavers had sold her to the madam who ran this wretched place. She licked her dry lips and refused to cry.

You are strong. You are the daughter of a shah and an English lady. No one owns you—no matter what happens tonight.

It was the mantra she had spoken again and again as the slavers had mocked her during their long days at sea. She hadn't been the only woman they'd captured, but she'd been one of the few they had left unspoiled. Her father's name had carried weight enough to give her that protection, at least so far as the greed of the men was concerned.

"Sell a Persian princess and turn a tidy profit." She could still hear the sneering voice of the captain as he'd coiled a lock of her hair around his fingers and crushed her breasts with his exploring hands before they'd thrown her in a tiny chamber, where she'd spent the next two weeks of their voyage.

Now Zehra Darzi stared at the locked door that kept her trapped in her new prison. Through the thin walls of the gaudy bedchamber she could hear the sounds of passion, of men grunting and women moaning along with the heavy sounds of furniture moving rhythmically. Bile rose in her mouth again. She tried not to think of how this tiny room was so different from the colorful, open rooms and rose gardens she'd once called home.

At least you escaped Al-Zahrani. He cannot find you here. She hoped that was true. He had bragged during her brief captivity that he engaged in slavery, like many powerful men in the area, and he'd once told her that the Western countries paid handsomely for foreign beauties. He'd assured her that he would never sell her, however, because he wanted the pleasure of breaking her spirit himself.

No man would *ever* break her spirit.

Zehra glared at the blasted door handle, wishing it would magically unlock, but even then, she knew escape would be impossible. When she'd been escorted to this room, two strong men had stood guard outside, their expressionless faces frightening. She doubted they had moved since.

For the tenth time since she'd been cast into this bedchamber, she eased down on the bed and tried to calm the fear that rolled through her. She couldn't sit still while her life and freedom hung in the balance. Zehra ran through her options. She had attempted bribery, but the madam and her gaggle of whores had laughed when Zehra had promised riches beyond their wildest dreams. She was coldly informed that her only value was the money she would bring at a private auction tonight. When Zehra had told her she was half-English, with relatives in the peerage, they had laughed again, clearly disbelieving. Her skin was too olive in color, her hair raven black, and her features more exotic. She was no English rose in their eyes.

I may be a woman, but I will fight before I surrender to despair.

Her one last hope—a dim, if not impossible one—was to find a gentleman from tonight's auction who would listen to her and believe her when she told him she was here against her will. She could not be a slave, for slavery was outlawed in England. Of course, the madam had reminded her that even the English kept their dark secrets, like slaves, but surely there would be one man tonight who would have mercy and set her free.

The door handle clicked as the lock turned. Zehra braced herself against the bedpost, fingers digging into the wood. She blew out a breath in relief as a woman in a curly blonde wig sauntered inside. The rouge coloring over the white paste on her cheeks matched the beautiful red dress she held.

"The madam says you're ta wear this tonight. I'm ta help ya." The woman set the gown on the bed and placed her hands on her hips. "No funny business, mind. The guards are outside, and they'll catch ya right quick if ya try to run."

Zehra studied the woman's pale face. Her scraggly blonde wig was pulled back into a messy coiffure, and her arms were thin. Her body was slim, but in a sickly sort of way. Zehra was a strong, full-figured woman. It would be easy to overpower her, but not the guards outside.

"I *said* no funny business," the woman snapped. "I see you lookin' toward the door. Gowan, get on with it." She waved at the dress, which she'd tossed on the bed.

"Very well." Zehra reached for the buttons on the front of her dress and began to slip them out of the little slits. The woman waited until Zehra had stepped out of her pale-blue traveling dress before helping her into the red satin evening gown. It fit well enough on Zehra's curvy figure, but the moment it was on, a wave of nausea overtook her. She closed her eyes, taking slow deep breaths until the sick feeling had passed.

"'At'll do, won't it?" The woman nodded at Zehra.

Zehra studied her reflection in the mirror in the corner by the locked window. The red silk set off the light-olive tint of her skin, but the bodice was scandalously low. She had been raised in a land where women did not dress like this, and she knew from her mother that English women did not wear necklines this low, either.

"The shoes will have to do." The blonde woman stared down at Zehra's sensible black boots. "And your hair—ain't nobody here can style it like them fine ladies do."

Though she had her mother's bright-blue eyes and full lips, Zehra's Persian features and raven-black hair had been inherited from her father. She had pulled her hair up with pins in a loose tumble days ago while still confined to the cabin aboard the ship, and she hadn't touched it since. She hastily adjusted the pins now.

"'Tis fine. Won't matter in a few hours. Not when you'll be on your back giving it up to some fine gent. Probably goin' to be that dark-skinned fella." The woman was prattling on, and Zehra was barely listening until she heard the words "dark-skinned."

She grasped the woman's arm. "What? What man?"

The prostitute scowled, and Zehra released her. "Some man was talking to the madam about you. He's darker than you are.

Found out you'd been sold here, and he tried to buy you straightaway. Said you belonged to him."

Al-Zahrani's words knifed through that thin veil of hope she'd been clinging to. *"You belong to me."*

"What did he say, exactly? Did he mention his name?"

"Name? I didn't 'ear that. Something foreign, funny, you know." The woman plucked at her gown, but the wrinkled fabric was beyond saving. "He's come before, that one. Sells girls like you all the time. Doesn't usually buy, though. He was right mad someone else had sold you to us. The madam told him he had to bid at the auction like everyone else."

No...oh, heavens no. It was Al-Zahrani. It had to be. A strange rust taste filled her mouth, and sweat coated her palms. He was going to buy her tonight. He would pay anything for her. And then...

"Right, come with me." The woman started for the door, and Zehra followed behind, touching the small gold locket around her throat. It was the only thing of value she had left, and it held her parents' portraits inside. Al-Zahrani had seen no advantage in taking it from her when he'd kidnapped her, and the slavers on the ship hadn't known she'd hidden it away in her skirts. The gold was warm upon her skin, and she traced the intricate floral patterns, wishing more than anything that her parents were still alive, that she was still asleep in her bed, having an awful nightmare.

The brothel was decorated with red satin wallpaper. Gilded sconces illuminated the hall as the prostitute led Zehra to a door at the end of the corridor. Three tall, muscled servants stood behind her, preventing any chance of escape. Zehra fisted her hands in the folds of her skirts to keep them from shaking. The door opened, and a flood of sound hit her. Men were laughing and talking in the dark interior of the room beyond. There was a small stage with a chair on it. Somewhere in the darkness, Al-Zahrani was likely waiting, like a wolf preparing to pounce.

The blonde-haired woman nudged her toward the stage. "Go and sit down." Zehra kept her head down, even though she couldn't see any of the men because of the lighting on the stage.

"Well, we start tonight's auction with a treat for you gentlemen." An Englishman spoke, then chuckled. "Feast your eyes upon this Persian princess. What pleasures might this virginal beauty know in your bed? Bidding starts at five hundred pounds."

Her heart pounded as the men began to bid. The numbers climbed higher and higher. The heavy scents of tobacco and spirits hung in the air, filling her nose with a stench she couldn't bear. She saw the shadows of men just behind the reach of the chandelier's glow. They prowled at the edges of her vision like creatures born of shadows. Harsh laughter echoed around the room, providing a ghoulish symphony to the sounds of the brothel. She focused on the bidding, trying to fight off her panic by reciting the numbers in her head over and over.

"Two thousand pounds!" Al-Zahrani's voice carried across the room. There was no mistaking it. Zehra didn't move, didn't flinch, even though part of her had turned to ice.

Please, let someone bid against him. The devil himself would be preferable.

"Two thousand?" A silken voice from nearby chuckled. "Heavens, this beauty is worth more than that! Seven thousand!"

She almost looked up, wondering who would spend so much to be her master, but she didn't. She would only stare out into darkness and see nothing. Would Al-Zahrani bid against this other man?

Please, let this devil win, whoever he is. I would rather him be my master.

There was a hush in the room as the man who'd bid seven thousand pounds laughed. "No one brave enough to bid higher, eh?" That voice, like a warm fire in winter, made her skin flush.

The man running the auction stepped closer to the stage. "Any other bids? Seven thousand going once..." He paused for an eternity. "Going twice..."

Zehra couldn't breathe. "*Sold* to the gentleman bidder for seven thousand pounds. Once you have paid for your lady, you may take her with you."

Zehra finally looked up, peering hopelessly into the darkness around her, but she saw only dim shapes.

"This way." The auctioneer gripped her arm cruelly and dragged her from the stage, ignoring her cry. She stumbled.

"Stop that!" a man snarled from close beside her as a hand gripped her other arm, firm but gentle, trying to steady her.

"You harm her again and I will cut you down, you understand? I don't want my property damaged."

"Of course." The auctioneer hastily loosened his grip. Zehra knew she would have bruises on the morrow.

"Are you all right, my dear?" the man asked. She squinted in the darkness, her eyes slowly adjusting. She caught sight of a tall handsome man with red hair. She'd prayed for a devil to rescue her, and she'd found one. She glanced around, afraid she would spy Al-Zahrani waiting to steal her away.

"Yes...I..." She swallowed, unsure what else to say.

"Good. Wait for me. I won't be long. I promise not to let anyone hurt you." The man turned and vanished into the crowd.

He wouldn't let anyone hurt her? She felt a surge of hope inside her so strong that she almost smiled. He had mercy, this beautiful stranger. He could be the one to set her free, and then she might find her mother's family.

"Come, this way," the auctioneer growled and once more took her arm, though less rough than before, and escorted her back to her chamber. Zehra barely heard the man's grumbling—all she could think about was that tonight might not be as awful as she'd feared. If she could just convince the man who'd bought her to help her, she might yet survive.

"He'll come for you once he's paid." The man chuckled.

"Assuming he has that much money. No gent's ever paid that much for a pretty bird like you. I hope you're worth it, because the madam won't be giving anyone their money back." The auctioneer laughed softly, the sound grating on her ears as he shut the chamber door in her face.

Zehra swallowed hard. The finality of the sound of the lock clicking into place still filled her with dread, but she clung to the hope her rescuer had given her. Zehra pressed her forehead against the wood, catching her breath and trying not to cry. She was afraid and hopeful and so exhausted, but perhaps tonight everything would be all right.

Please... Let him be a man of mercy and save me from Al-Zahrani.

~

Lawrence Russell despised the White House in Soho. It was one of the less reputable brothels in London, and it had a dark side that made even a seasoned rogue such as himself shudder in revulsion. His tastes ran more toward the Midnight Garden, which catered less to hired pleasure workers and more toward matching aristo-cratic ladies and gentlemen with similar needs.

When I seduce a woman, it is out of mutual desire, not a monetary transaction.

No mistress he'd ever had demanded fine clothes or jewels—they'd only begged him never to leave their beds. He'd been quite happy to oblige for as long as he could.

He stared around at the crowd in the dimly lit card room. The tables had been pushed back half a dozen feet to make room for a small stage, large enough to accommodate a person in the chair that had been placed in the center. The room was filled with men, smoke drifting lazily from lit cigars as they talked and drank. There were quite a few faces he recognized. Thankfully, none whom he considered to be close friends. Tonight's auction and the very idea of it turned Lawrence's stomach.

He wouldn't be here at all except for the letter he'd received from his younger brother, Avery, telling him to go tonight and take note of which men bought the merchandise from tonight's private auction.

What Lawrence hadn't realized was that the merchandise was to be *slaves*. He'd hoped it might have been some other disreputable activity he was helping to stop, but slavery? Not just any slavery, but that of an intimate nature.

Slavery had been outlawed in England, at least publicly. Yet women would be sold to the highest bidder here tonight like horses at Tattersall's, and no doubt treated less kindly. His blood boiled at the very thought of women facing such a fate. He *adored* women. Women were lovely, delicate creatures who deserved kind, playful, and rewarding lovers in bed. Not this injustice.

From the moment he'd heard the whispers from other men in this room, his heart had begun to fill with dread. Avery was supposed to arrive just after the auction to stop the men who purchased these women and have them arrested.

But what if Avery arrived too late? What if some of the men were able to leave before the auction concluded and the women weren't able to be saved? A hundred new fears rose up inside him as he tried to focus and remain calm. He had to catalogue every man in this room who bid, not only those who purchased a slave.

One of the men who ran the White House approached the stage and adjusted the small but elegant chair on the stage. A hush settled over the crowd, and a tension built in the air so thick that Lawrence could feel it choking him.

"We will be starting shortly, gentlemen. Please be patient." The hum of the conversations around him returned. He had time yet before the auction began. Lawrence leaned back against the wall, next to the closest door that would give him a quick exit. He wanted to leave the moment this dreadful scene was over.

The door beside him creaked open, and a dirty blonde-haired woman led a woman dressed in red into the room. They passed close to him as they approached the stage. Satin whispered against his boots as the second woman brushed past him. A hint of rose-water teased his nose. He watched her progress toward the stage, following her movements, hating that this woman faced the fate that she did. It was enough to make any decent man sick.

Lawrence sucked in a breath as the light bathed the woman when she drew near the small dais. Men leered and several called out cruel suggestions of what they'd like to do to her. Lawrence moved toward her and the stage as if in a dream. Her raven-black hair and light-olive skin were exquisite, even beneath the glare of the single chandelier over her head. The red satin dress she wore clung to every curve, leaving little to the imagination. Rather than looking cheap, the woman looked irresistible.

Whispers stirred in the men around him as they stared hungrily at the item they soon planned to bid for. Lawrence fought the urge to run for the woman, grab her, and flee after he'd shoved every man in the room off a very high cliff.

As she lifted her skirts to climb the dais, he caught a sight of sensible black boots that covered her slender ankles. His body flared to life, and he was ashamed at his own arousal.

Don't look at her—look at the men. It's them you must remember.

He began to turn his focus away from the woman, but then he saw her face. His heart stilled in his chest. It was as though everything around him had frozen, locked between one breath and the next as his gaze became transfixed on the woman's face. There was something about her feminine, exotic features that drew him in. She had slightly softened high cheekbones, a sensual mouth, winged brows, and shocking blue eyes that were so bright they gleamed like sapphires in the light that illuminated her face.

Something stirred deep in his mind like fragments of a long-forgotten dream, or perhaps the strands of a partially unbound tapestry. Was it possible to recognize someone he'd never met? The queer feeling didn't subside, and that puzzled him. He'd never met her—he was sure of it—but why then did he feel as though he had? Or *hadn't...*

Damnation, he couldn't make sense of what his mind and memory were trying to tell him.

One of the White House employees stood close to the stage. "We start tonight's auction with a treat for you gentlemen." His words and the luscious beauty on the stage captured every man's attention.

"Feast your eyes upon this Persian princess. What pleasures might this virginal beauty know in your bed? Bidding starts at five hundred pounds."

Lawrence swallowed hard as men around him began to bid.

You must not interfere. You must not.

It was all too familiar. He realized he wasn't recognizing the woman, but the feelings surrounding this travesty. The fear, the panic, his own impotence to do anything to stop it. He'd been too young then, too young and too late to save a woman who had needed someone's help. Anyone's help. *His* help.

I won't let it happen again.

He stared at the woman on the stage, taking in her pale, stoic face as she listened to the sounds of men who would claim her. Her hands, clutching her skirts, shook ever so slightly. She had to be terrified yet was hiding it well. He couldn't help but admire her. In that moment he made a decision.

I can't leave her to these wolves. I won't let the past repeat itself.

He had to act. His brother's warnings to only watch and observe be damned. Lawrence glanced at the woman, forcing himself to hide his anxiety and become the relaxed scandalous rogue the rest of the world knew. He had to play the part convincingly, or else he risked losing her to another man.

Hold on, darling. I'll save you.

CHAPTER 2

L awrence didn't want to participate in this dreadful slave auction. But if the lady went home with one of these men, they would force her to do things she didn't want, and he couldn't stand the thought of that.

When he'd been only seventeen, not yet truly a man, he'd ventured into a brothel much like this. He'd thought himself a virile and entitled lad, eager to see himself pleasured for as much as his coin purse would allow. His head had been filled with images of eager maids feeding him berries on a lounge, willingly submitting to his overtures, and everyone partaking in a night none would soon forget.

Instead, he'd watched women selling themselves to survive. It wasn't hard to see the desperation in the performances of those who didn't want to be there, or the emptiness of those who had given up and knew no other life. What was worse were the men who treated them no better than cattle.

That night he'd watched a woman, boldly announced by the haggard proprietor as working her very first night, dragged away by some brute who'd paid to be the first to have her. She'd begged him not to, saying that she was there against her will, but he'd struck her across the face before they'd even left the room. He'd heard the men around him laughing at her misfortune. He'd been frozen, unable to intervene, too young and afraid. It had haunted him every moment since then.

He'd run from that place, sickened by everything it stood for and he'd never told a soul about his secret shame. It wasn't until he learned of the Midnight Garden and its courtesans that he discovered better establishments existed, but nonetheless the experience had soured his taste for paid companionship forever.

"Two thousand pounds!" a man close to the stage called out. The bold offer shook Lawrence back to reality. He moved closer to better see the fellow. With dark hair, olive skin, and a deep accent, he was surely no native to England. The man stared at the woman with a hungry fixation, and Lawrence shuddered. The hint of cruelty that hung about his cold smile made Lawrence's blood run cold, taking him back to that night in the brothel long ago. He could not let this man have her. He would not.

Lawrence stepped forward and managed a chuckle. "Two thousand? Heavens, this beauty is worth more than that! Seven thousand!"

He pushed off from the wall he'd been leaning against and walked over to stand closer to the stage, forcing several others out of his way. Lawrence had to make a statement to the rest of the room or else face a bidding war he might not win.

A hush fell upon the crowd, but Lawrence focused only on the woman sitting on the stage. He had to be the one to take her home and set her free.

"No one brave enough to bid higher, eh?" he said, as confidently as he could possibly present himself. Not one of them responded, not even a murmur. He could have dropped a feather and the sound would have reverberated around the room like cannon fire.

"Any other bids?" the auctioneer asked the room. "Seven thousand going once..." Lawrence hands curled into fists. "Going twice..."

The woman on the stage wasn't breathing, her face etched in stone. She must be terrified. *Hold on, darling. Just a few seconds more.*

The auctioneer's face lit with greed as he pointed to Lawrence. "*Sold* to the gentleman bidder for seven thousand pounds. Once you have paid for your lady, you may take her with you."

The woman looked up, seeking him out, and Lawrence stepped closer, wishing she could see his face and not be afraid. The auctioneer grabbed her arm and dragged her off the stage. Lawrence saw her stumble, a flash of fear in those stunning eyes, and he reacted instantly.

"Stop that!" he bellowed and gripped the woman's other arm gently. He glowered at the auctioneer. "You harm her again and I will cut you down, you understand? I don't want my property damaged."

"Of course." The auctioneer's face turned ashen, and rightly so. Lawrence's blood was boiling with fury.

He turned his attention to the woman to let his temper cool. "Are you all right, my dear?"

She squinted up at him, and he realized the bright lights hanging over the stage had likely made it hard for her to see.

"Yes... I..." Her voice was silken, yet each word vibrated with fear.

"Good. Wait for me. I won't be long. I promise not to let anyone hurt you."

He reluctantly let go of her arm and strode to the back of the room, where another door led to the madam's office. A plump woman was seated at a desk, writing names and numbers in a ledger. She barely glanced at him when he entered. "I've come to pay for my"—he choked on the next word—"merchandise."

"Oh?" The woman finally glanced up. Her dark eyes fixed on

him, taking in his fine clothes as though assessing his ability to pay.

"Yes, here's a banknote." He set out a hefty sum, knowing he was good for it. As the second son of a marquess, he had learned early on about the importance of investing. He had no desire to beg his older brother, Lucien, for money. Lucien would give him anything he asked for, but Lawrence had his pride.

"Thank you." The madam collected the note and waved a hand at him in dismissal. It was obvious he merited no more attention than it took to process his purchase. The White House was vastly different from the Midnight Garden—no warm embrace of Madame Chanson as she greeted guests to be found here. She ran her house entirely on referrals and only hired ladies and gentlemen who were professionals, not those desperate for coin. They were true *cortigiane oneste*, skilled in far more than matters of the flesh. London's elite chose the Midnight Garden when they wanted their pleasures clean and without what Lawrence called "sullied waters." This was not in reference to the ladies, but rather the men who frequented those establishments and the diseases they often spread.

Lawrence exited the madam's office and spotted the dirty-haired blonde who had escorted his woman to the stage.

"Excuse me, miss. Could you please take me to the room of the woman I…" Again he swallowed the distasteful words.

"Bought?" the woman supplied with a knowing grin. Lawrence frowned, but nodded.

"This way, lovey. She's a *real* beauty, that one. But keep your knives and pistols out of reach, if you know what I mean. She's got a fire in her eyes. She'll likely try to slit your throat the moment you fall asleep."

Lawrence unconsciously reached up and fussed with his cravat as they came to a door at the end of the hall. The woman slipped an old brass key into the lock, turning it until it clicked, and then she stepped back out of the way, allowing him entrance. He closed the door behind himself and spotted the woman on the opposite side of the room.

She had placed the bed between them. Her hands were slightly raised, as though she would strike out in self-defense at any moment. He was torn between disappointment at her fear and admiration for her fire. A woman who fought for herself was a woman to be respected.

He lifted his own palms. "Be at ease, darling. I'm not going to hurt you. I didn't even plan on…" She stared at him, her blue eyes so striking that he lost his train of thought. He recovered himself. "What is your name?" he asked.

The woman was silent for a long moment. "Zehra Darzi."

"Miss Darzi, I am Lawrence Russell." He took a step closer, and she stepped back like a skittish colt, but her eyes promised danger if he continued.

"As I said, I have no desire to harm you."

"So you say." She spoke English well, but she also had a rich accent he couldn't quite place. The foreign touch made her voice enchanting and mysterious.

"Rest assured, my word is my bond. I bought you to save you from the other men. I will not take advantage of you. Now or ever."

Zehra raised a dark brow. "A hot-blooded man with an angelic face wishes *not* to take me to bed? I do not know if I believe you. Beautiful men such as you *always* wish to bed women."

He couldn't resist grinning. "You think I'm beautiful?" He knew of his appeal to the fairer sex, but to hear it from this woman felt like more than just flattery.

"You know you are, Mr. Russell."

He tilted his head, studying her. *"With hair dark as a raven's wing, and eyes like polished moonstones, she sweeps me away on dreams of morning mists."* He quoted an old poem, one he barely remembered except for that single line.

"'The Raven Lass'?" she asked. "William Helms. An obscure poem, is it not?"

"Indeed," he said, stunned she would even know it. "One of my mother's favorites. She often recited it to me as a boy, but I'll be damned if I can remember any more of it."

"My mother also taught me this poem," Zehra murmured, her enchanting blue eyes darkened as she stared at him.

"Oh? What a curious thing. I—"

Whatever he'd planned to say was cut short by the sounds of a commotion outside. He opened the door and saw several prostitutes fleeing down the hall. One of them was the blonde who had brought him here. He caught her arm as she ran past.

"What's the matter?"

"Bow Street Runners! They're raiding the house. You'd best get out right quick. They'll send your woman back on the boat if they find her here." The woman ripped free of his grasp and fled down the hall.

"About damned time!" Lawrence muttered. The Runners would find them, and he could return Zehra to her home—or at least, they would see her back onto a ship that would take her there.

"*Please.*" Zehra's voice came from directly behind him. As he turned around, her hand caught his arm, her grip surprisingly strong. "Please, do not let them send me back. I will go home with you." Her imploring gaze was nearly impossible to deny.

"But you will be safe and—"

She shook her head. "No, I will not. I must stay here. With you."

There was more shouting from outside their door. Lawrence had only seconds to decide what he was going to do.

"You won't be safe going back?"

She shook her head, but did not explain herself.

"You truly wish to stay with me?"

"Yes. If you are a man of your word." She gave his palm another squeeze, and he returned it.

"Very well, be quick and quiet. We must get past the men. If we can reach the street, I may be able to get you out without being detected."

He held her hand, relishing her warm skin against his as they rushed down the corridor in the same direction the flock of light-skirts had gone earlier. Several rooms' doors were open, and men were rushing to clothe themselves. Some were climbing out windows.

Lawrence found a door that opened to the gardens in the back. "This way."

"Are you sure?" Zehra asked.

"Positive." At least he hoped so. He'd had to flee many a house via the gardens ever since he'd been old enough to seduce ladies. This wasn't the first time he'd scaled a hedge or battled through rosebushes and rhododendrons. He and Zehra crept through the darkened maze of bushes until they found their way into the mews between the White House and the edifice next to it.

"Wait here while I find a hackney." He nudged her into the shadows, and she flattened herself against the wall. For a moment their eyes locked, and he could see her fear and trust warring with each other.

"Shouldn't you hurry?" she asked in a shaky whisper.

"Right," he muttered and rushed down the alley to the street.

∽

Zehra held her breath as she waited in the shadows. The bushes around her rustled as she listened, fighting the urge to flee. And then she heard *his* voice.

"The impertinence. The *arrogance*. It will not go unpunished. I will find her. That man who bought her will have signed his name to the madam's book. We will come tomorrow, and I will discover his name, and when I find him..." The voice sank to a low growl. "I will cut his throat and take back what is mine."

"Aye, sir," another man responded, carrying a rough English accent. "But wouldna that be dangerous? Cuttin' a man's throat? You could be caught and hanged."

Al-Zahrani's voice rippled through the bushes, and Zehra closed her eyes, fighting the urge to run and give herself away.

"I'll kill any who stand in my way, do you understand? She has family here. No doubt she will go to them eventually. Have men watch their home, night and day. Report anything unusual. The moment I find her, I will take her by any means necessary."

No... Zehra's eyes began to well. He would kill innocent men and women to get to her, her own family. A family who might not even know she existed. Zehra pressed herself deeper into the tall bushes, willing herself to not exist in that moment.

Don't let him find me, please. She begged the heavens to grant her this one favor if nothing else.

Al-Zahrani and his man moved farther away, but she dared not move. She prayed Lawrence would come and find her soon.

~

Lawrence skidded to a halt as he reached the pavement. A number of Bow Street Runners were still on the steps of the White House.

"Bloody hell." He waited, watching the men for what felt like an eternity before they joined the others inside the brothel.

"About time." He walked briskly down the street, trying to look inconspicuous, which was difficult at midnight. He found a coach ready to take on passengers and waved for the man to come down the alley to him. Then he slipped back into the alley to find Zehra. She was waiting right where he'd left her. When he got close enough to reach for her hand, he noticed she was trembling.

"You must be freezing." He removed his coat and slid it over her shoulders before she could protest. "This way. I found a coach.

We must move quickly if we are to get inside without being seen." He slipped her arm in his and led her to the coach. Before they climbed inside, he caught her chin and tilted it up to his. "Understand, you don't have to come with me. You are free to leave. Do you have friends here? Anyone who could take you in? I'd be happy to take you anywhere you wish to go."

Zehra reached for his hand, and the gesture made his blood pound. "My lord, I *want* to come with you. You must believe me— it is far safer this way."

He shouldn't be feeling so attached to her. Not like this. Yet her words moved him all the same. "Very well. Quickly, get inside." He helped her into the coach and gave the driver his address, and it began to rattle down the street. Lawrence breathed a sigh of relief as Zehra sat beside him. Without thinking, he curled an arm around her shoulders and tucked her against his side. She stiffened a moment but then relaxed, and he enjoyed the feel of her feminine form so close to him. Her lips parted and her hands clenched in her skirts as she leaned toward the window, peering through the curtains. Her eyes were fixed on the streets.

"It is so different here," she murmured.

"Different?" he asked, curious.

"Yes." She pointed at the moonlit streets, and despite her blush, there was a fire and steadiness in her voice and gaze as she spoke.

"Please, tell me what you meant to say." He wanted her to speak. That soft voice of hers was heaven-sent, and he could've listened to her talk for hours. He usually liked to hear women sigh or moan his name, but from Zehra he wanted conversation. He sensed that anything she said would have meaning.

"It's so cold and harsh here. My home was warm and colorful."

"Where is your home?" he asked, half afraid she wouldn't tell him.

"Persia," she replied softly.

He blinked. "Wait, the auctioneer wasn't lying? You really are from Persia?" She nodded, and he smiled. "Does that mean you are a princess too?"

"Perhaps," she replied, a soft twinkle in her eyes.

She seemed so afraid, so hesitant around him, but he understood. She was a brave woman facing a life as a slave if she couldn't trust him. He was about to ask her why she wanted to stay here with him, but the coach rolled to a stop and the driver announced his address. He moved to get out first and relished lifting her down from the coach. Nothing seemed more wonderful than holding her close in his arms, and he hated having to set her down on the ground and let go.

With a furtive glance about, he saw the street was empty, so they rushed up the steps to his door. His butler, Mr. MacTavish, was waiting for him. The old stout Scotsman's eyes widened at the sight of Zehra, but he did not question her presence. Lawrence had kept a fair number of mistresses in recent years, which meant a lady after midnight was not completely unexpected. They didn't usually stay for more than a night, so MacTavish would likely be surprised by Zehra staying longer.

"MacTavish, this is Miss Zehra Darzi, and she is my esteemed guest. Please have a chamber prepared for her."

The old Scotsman blinked in momentary confusion. "Not your room?" he queried, his tone polite and careful.

"No. Miss Darzi will have her own chambers. She will advise you what her needs are with regard to meals and anything else."

Lawrence paused at the base of the stairs, Zehra at his side as he looked at her. "You do not have a maid... I've only just realized you must have nothing. How foolish of me."

Zehra shook her head. "I had a maid back home, of course, but she was..." Her words trailed off. She seemed to consider her next words carefully. "She is no longer with me."

MacTavish interjected. "Er... Shall I make inquiries first thing in the morning to procure a maid for the lady?"

Lawrence replied, "Yes," at the same time Zehra said, "No."

"You will have need of a maid while you remain here,"

Lawrence explained. "I can't ask my upstairs maids to spend time away from their duties to assist you. I would much prefer you have a maid ready to see to your every need, not to mention your changes of clothes."

Her cheeks pinkened, and she glanced away. "I have only this gown. A maid shall not be needed."

Lawrence gaped at her. "Zehra, you wound me." He was teasing, but the flash of panic in her eyes made him move on hastily. "You have met me under the *least* reputable circumstances, I know, but rest assured you will be treated properly under my roof." He stroked her cheek, loving the way her eyes dilated. "That means, I'm afraid, that you must endure a new wardrobe."

Zehra stared at him in disbelief as he led her upstairs. Below them, MacTavish called for servants to attend to them.

"You may rest in my chambers for now until they have your room prepared." He escorted her to his own room and ushered her inside. A fire was lit, and Lawrence knew a tray of food would soon be sent up, but for now at least, he could get Zehra settled. She lingered by the door, her elegant fingers twining in the silk of her gown. Lawrence longed to reach out and touch those hands again, to reassure her that all was well, but he feared she still did not trust him.

"Please, sit. I can offer you wine or a bit of brandy?" He started toward the decanters on his side table, then his face turned a ruddy red. "I suppose you don't drink spirits do you? I apologize if I caused any offense.

"No, it's fine. I do drink occasionally. My mother wasn't Persian and I was raised in two different cultures. I would like a glass of wine please," Zehra replied as she seated herself in the first chair by the fire. He poured her a glass and handed it to her, then sat in the chair watching her. She gulped heavily. Her father would have disapproved but her mother had often let her have a glass of wine in secret when it was just the two of them and Zehra was quite partial to it.

"Did they provide you with enough sustenance at the White House?"

"The White House?" she asked, confused.

"Yes, the brothel where you..."

"Oh." Her cheeks turned dark red. "A little. I had a glass of water and a piece of bread around midday—"

"God's teeth!" Lawrence cursed. The poor woman had been starved. She jumped at his outburst. "My apologies. I didn't mean to startle you. It's just that the more I learn of this place the more furious it makes me." That wasn't nearly a strong enough word, but he wasn't about to tell this poor frightened woman he wanted to go back and raze the place to the ground.

Zehra sipped her wine more slowly, her eyes locked on his as though seeking to ascertain if he was still a threat. She ought to have a minute alone, even from him. It might give her time to adjust and feel safer.

"I think I'll go down and have some extra food brought up. Please stay here and warm yourself by the fire."

He left her alone, feeling she could do with a bit of quiet after the horrors she'd suffered. It was clear from her speech that she was a highborn lady and not used to the treatment she'd endured. Not that *any* woman should be used to it. MacTavish was in the hallway waiting for him, his dark brows drawn together in concern.

"My lord, is she... Does she need anything?"

"Yes. Food. Have everything Cook can make sent up at once."

His butler nodded, and by MacTavish's hesitation it was clear that he sensed Zehra was not a typical guest.

"I shall explain everything to you once it's safe. It is for her sake, not mine, that we must have secrecy."

MacTavish nodded. He'd served Lawrence since Lawrence had turned twenty and was no stranger to taking orders of a peculiar nature. "The maids will see to her room, and I will let everyone know that this guest is special and her presence a secret."

"Thank you. Apologize to everyone for the late hour." Lawrence walked downstairs to his study, where he pulled out a bit of parchment and prepared a quill and fresh ink pot. He hesitated, however, when he put his quill tip down.

What would he say to his brother? Apologize for buying a woman when he'd vowed he would not interfere? Yet what should he have done? Sit idly by as a woman had her freedom stripped from her? If anything, it was his brother's fault for not properly warning him.

He had taken one look at Zehra and knew he couldn't let her be taken by another man. There was something about her eyes and how she moved. It brought back memories so far in the recesses of his mind, and they seemed to whisper to him, but he couldn't pull them into the light, couldn't make sense of what he was seeing—or half remembering.

Yes, there was something about Zehra that he could not get out of his mind. She reminded him too much of the young woman from the brothel years before, though not directly in looks, of course. It was the situation as a whole. It felt as though he'd been given a second chance to right a past wrong.

He stared hard at the parchment. With a curse, he crumpled it into a ball and tossed it into the fire. As he watched the embers eat away at it, he sighed and looked up at the ceiling to where Zehra sat now, one floor above.

She was a lovely woman who'd been through a horrifying ordeal, and he was moved by her in ways that were far too dangerous. He'd never considered himself a true gentleman—he took after his older brother, Lucien, far too much. As his mother had said more than once, "Rogues run in the family." If he kept Zehra under his roof for very long, he would have trouble remaining a gentleman.

Yet he was not a man who ever forced seduction on any woman, either. He did have some scruples he still clung to, by God. But if she gave him any indication she wished to share his bed, he most certainly would not turn her down. The problem would be in determining if such a request was genuine or out of some sense of obligation. He wouldn't abide the latter.

Lawrence leaned back in his chair, frowning. This week his entire family was to be present for various summer parties in London, and he would no doubt be forced to attend these events as well, but what of Zehra?

He would have to keep his Persian princess safely tucked away for now. He could still see the look of fear in her eyes as she begged him to keep her, even though he'd promised her freedom. Something had frightened her about being returned home. It was a mystery—one he had every intention of getting to the bottom of once she had a chance to rest.

Lord, he was thankful no other man had bid against him. Seven thousand was an unbelievable sum, one he would have trouble explaining should anyone question his accounts—that was assuming the White House was able to use it, which was unlikely given that the Bow Street Runners were tearing the brothel apart. But he had won, and he was relieved she'd come home with him. She was safe now and would remain so under his watch.

CHAPTER 3

Z ehra sipped her wine, even though her belly quivered with an ache born of days with little to no food. She fought to ignore the beating headache rising in her head by examining the bedchamber of her rescuer. His tall four-poster bed with a dark-green coverlet looked inviting, perhaps too much so. He had a shaving stand, complete with a washbasin, and a chest of drawers. A tall bookcase stood against one wall, and it was filled with books, some old, others quite new. She carried her wine glass with her as she approached the shelf.

"Who are you, Lawrence Russell?" she whispered, reading the gilded spines on the shelves. Gothic novels, poetry, sciences, art, philosophy. He was well-read, it seemed. Surely a man who was well-read was less likely to be a cruel man. At least, she hoped so.

He claimed he had bought her to protect her from other men. But she had learned the hard truth of late that she could trust no one—not strangers, not even friends. Her parents lay dead because they'd trusted a man they thought was their friend.

Zehra closed her eyes. Tears trickled down her face, and the cool spring air drifting through the open window dried the wet streaks. She mastered herself, bearing the pain of her loss. There would be a time to mourn, but not yet, not until she found her mother's family and learned if they would offer her a home or cast her out.

She could almost hear her father's voice. *"You must be strong a little while longer, my desert rose, just a little longer."* Desert rose. How often he'd called her that. Her mother had laughed with delight at the name whenever Zehra would dance in a puddle of colorful rose petals, breathing in the heady perfume of nature's finest flower.

For a moment, she was borne back into the past, and sunny memories swept her far from this dark, cold island. Her father sat before a fire in a pit, the night sky glittering with stars, as he played the setar, an instrument similar to an Indian sitar. He sang in a haunting voice. Zehra would sit wrapped in her mother's arms, as her mother whispered to her the words of her father's music.

I am a candle burning for you,
   My heart is aflame with ardor for you,
   Yet you shall never come home,
   My gleaming pearl, my dearest heart,
   I wait...I wait in the darkness, burning bright into the night,
   Hoping against hope you will find your way home.

She had been too young to understand the look between her parents then, the softening gazes, the intimate secrets that lingered in the air unspoken between them.

But that life was over. She would never find her way home because it was her home no longer. All that was left was a burned palace, blood coating the smooth floor tiles. The stain of evil in that place would never fade, not for her. Even if she could go back, she would never return to the palace.

Her eyes flew open when the bedchamber door creaked. She turned, expecting to see Lawrence, but instead saw a dark-haired maid carrying a tray of food. "Excuse me, miss, the master asked for food to be sent to you." The woman smiled, her countenance warm, and Zehra wiped her tears from her cheeks. She took a moment to collect herself, trying to paint a cheery smile upon her lips as she faced the servant.

The maid placed the tray on the table by the fireplace and lifted up a warm blanket. She gestured for Zehra to sit in one of the nearby chairs.

"You look dead on your feet, miss. Why don't you sit here? The master has a fine chair by the fire, and it'll do you some good to rest."

The tall wingback chair did look rather cozy, she had to admit. After she sat, the maid tucked the blanket around her lap.

"For the chill, miss," she explained. "It can get a bit drafty at night."

"Thank you," Zehra said, moved by the servant's thoughtfulness. Her mother had rarely talked of England, but she said that the servants in England were far different from those Zehra had grown up with. She'd been raised to be held in reverence by those around her, and they would not dream of speaking to her, but this woman had treated her in such a friendly way. Zehra liked it. It made her feel less alone, and right now that mattered more than anything.

"There's leek soup, some cold meats, and fruit. If you need anything else, just pull the bell cord by the bed and someone will be up to see to whatever you need." The maid offered another smile and left Zehra to eat.

She looked at the metal dome over the plate and pulled it off. The delicious scents that teased her nose came as such a relief. She felt like weeping all over again. She went straight for the meat, wanting to soothe her hunger pangs.

A few minutes later, she'd cleaned the plate and was mopping up the last bit of soup with a slice of bread. For the first time in a week, she felt full. She leaned back in the chair, warmed by the fire and blankets, a sense of peace overcoming her...

She wasn't sure how long she slept before she was jerked awake at the sensation of being moved. She struggled as panic overrode her rationality as memories of being bound and imprisoned on the slave ship came flooding back.

"Easy, love, it's only me. Your room has been prepared. I was simply going to take you there." The masculine voice was familiar, and she realized in her sleepy haze that it was Lawrence who was carrying her. "You will be left alone then, I promise."

"My lord, please, I cannot sleep alone. Not tonight." She clutched his shirt, curling her fingers into the fine fabric. She didn't know why she'd suddenly begged him to stay with her, but for some reason as he carried her, she'd felt sure he would not harm her.

His fine features were shadowed by flame, and she realized the room around them was dark. The lamps had been extinguished, and only the fire remained lit.

"You're welcome to my bed. I can have a cot brought up if you wish for a servant to stay with you for the night. Or myself, if you prefer." His eyes channeled the moonlight from the nearby window, making her breath catch with their bright intensity. In her own land the men she'd met had possessed dark eyes of a hundred different hues, yet this light color, like wheat mixed with emerald, was unlike anything she'd ever seen. Her own bright-blue eyes were rare, she knew, but she found the endless tumbling facets of green and brown in Lawrence's far more enchanting.

Lawrence cradled her to his chest as he walked to his bed and laid her down. Despite his kind offer, trying to reassure her that he desired nothing from her in return, his quick and uneven breaths betrayed him. It seemed he was struggling to remain the gentleman he claimed to be. Still, it said much of his character that he could fight these demons so well, and she did not wish to offend him.

"You would have my thanks if you would stay in this room for the night."

Lawrence nodded. "There are plenty of blankets, but if you get cold, I have more. I'll just stay here in the chair. Call if you need anything." He turned away, and Zehra had a moment to study his fine figure silhouetted against the firelight. Then she lay back in the bed for a brief moment before she realized her gown was too tight, her breathing shallow. The gown she'd worn on the slave ship had been more comfortable than this, likely because the slavers had wanted easy access to the women they took and didn't care for corsets or stays. She sat back up and tried to reach behind her to unbutton the gown, but she couldn't. With a shiver, she looked toward Lawrence, who was still facing the fire.

"My lord, I have no way to unbutton this gown. The ladies at the White House left me rather helpless." She eased off the bed and walked toward Lawrence. He swallowed hard, and she swore she heard him mutter a curse before he sighed.

"Yes, of course, how thoughtless of me. You mustn't sleep in that gown. Shall I call up a maid to help?"

Zehra thought of the late hour and winced. She didn't want to drag a maid from her bed. "No, we should let them sleep. I trust you, my lord."

"Trust me?" He chuckled ruefully. "Very well, then."

He twirled a finger, indicating for her to turn her back to him. She did, holding her breath as his fingers began to pull at the laces. She relaxed as the gown became loose against her bent arms and then fell to the floor. His sudden intake of breath made her blush and smile. There was a part of her that was boldly sensual, unafraid of such things in many ways. She was a virgin, but she was not uneducated in the ways of men and women.

"Please, Lord, don't tell me you need help with the stays."

Lawrence's voice was low and rough. She sensed she'd pushed him too far.

"No, I can manage. Thank you, my lord." She stepped out of the puddle of her gown and stripped out of her remaining clothes, leaving a pile of stays, slippers, and stockings on the floor. Clad only in her chemise, she climbed back into Lawrence's bed and settled in for the night. She was so exhausted that she only heard him wrestling with the chair and a small pillow for a few minutes before she surrendered to sleep.

~

Avery Russell stepped into the chaos of the White House, his eyes taking in the Bow Street Runners and the local magistrate, a man named John Dearborn, as they took statements from several brothel patrons. Three men were restrained by iron shackles and seated at a card table in the main gaming room.

"Russell." One of the Runners, a man called Sam Cady, nodded and spoke to Avery as he came over. "We've put a stop to the auction. Unfortunately, the madam threw her account books into the fire, destroying the names of the men who paid to attend. All of the ladies have been placed in an adjoining room, but..."

"But what?"

Cady shrugged his large shoulders and nodded toward the restrained group of men. "One of the gentlemen here swears another man bought a slave, the first one to be sold. He and the girl aren't here."

"Someone got away?" Avery's hands curled into fists as he thought of some poor woman being carried away to a place where no one would find her, where she would be abused and defiled, where she would most likely never leave.

"Did this talkative fellow give us a name?"

Cady shook his head.

"Which man was it?" Avery demanded. He headed toward the prisoners. Cady shadowed behind him.

"Bloke on the left, the young one."

Avery grabbed the man, who seemed close to Avery's age, and snarled into his face.

"Who took the first woman? Give me a name!"

The young man gasped as his chair was pushed back to balance on two legs. "I—I don't know, but I got a good look at him! I swear!" With his hands bound behind him, he would have a nasty fall if the chair toppled over, which was exactly what Avery wanted him to fear. A threat of violence could be more effective than actually using it. A man's imagination was his own worst enemy.

"What did he look like?" Avery growled.

"He looked like you!" The man screeched as his chair teetered on its back legs.

Avery froze. "What?"

"He looked like you," the man repeated. "Not exactly, mind. His hair was a darker red, but the face...very similar." The man stared at him, but Avery was no longer paying attention. He let the chair fall back on all four legs.

Lawrence. What the bloody hell had his older brother done? He had been sent to gather information about the auction, not participate!

"What is it?" Cady asked, flexing his hands into fists. "Do you know who he's on about?" Cady was a good man, but his brutish build and height made him a damned scary sight when angered.

Avery shook his head. If his brother had bought a slave, there had to be a damned good reason. Had Lawrence thought he could play the hero, imagining himself rescuing the poor woman?

The problem was, a magistrate would not see it that way. Buying a woman like this was enough to condemn any man. Thankfully, Avery had spent years as a spy for king and country.

He was used to controlling his reactions and finding ways out of impossible situations. He turned to Cady.

"Leave this to me. I'll find out who the man is, and when I do, there will be justice," he vowed. Cady nodded and returned to the other Runners, leaving Avery alone. Avery headed for the madam's office, wanting to see what was left of the ledgers. He saw a small fireplace against the back wall opposite the desk. Three fat ledgers with marbleboard bindings were still smoldering on the hearth. Ashes littered the ground beneath the grate where the ledgers had been tossed.

Avery knelt down and carefully peeled back the pages. Most of it was illegible, and some pages crumbled even as he turned them, but he could just make out a few names and numbers.

"No..." He whispered a curse as he pushed apart the last pages to see the names more clearly.

"Lawrence Russell – One item – £7,000."

Lawrence, what have you done? You damned fool.

Pulling out a match from his inner pocket, he re-lit the fire and tore out the final page, casting it into the flames. There could be no evidence, no trace of his brother's actions.

I will fix it. I will find the woman and protect my family's name. No one need ever know about this.

He turned and left the madam's office. The magistrate was in charge of the scene now, and Avery could easily disappear into the darkness. He had reports to make. His superior, Sir Hugo Waverly, would need to be informed of the success of the breakup of the slave ring. With several influential Arab and Persian ambassadors in London for secret peace talks to stem the war between the Ottoman and the Qajar empires, it was crucial that this event never be discovered.

Avery slipped out of the White House and called for his horse. He needed to get home and rest, but come morning, he would go to Lawrence's home and demand answers. He would also have to take the poor woman to the port at once with the rest of the women and ship her home.

He only hoped he could keep Lawrence from facing the law if his brother had done something so foolish as to truly buy a slave. He would be hard pressed to save his brother if that was the case.

∽

Zehra couldn't wash the blood off her hands. The palace halls were filled with screams, and the night sky was illuminated with fire. Smoke crept along the corridors, prowling for victims. Bodies littered the bedroom and antechamber.

Zehra stared in shock at the two bodies closest to the bed. Her mother lay still, her golden hair spread across the silk sheets, her throat slashed. Blood pooled beneath her neck, and her sightless blue eyes looked through Zehra into oblivion.

A tall dark-haired man lay at her feet, his body still, a scimitar grasped in one hand. He had killed four men before being cut down.

Papa...the word didn't escape her lips, but it was followed inside her head by a piercing scream of anguish.

Later she could move again, and then she was sprinting down the corridor, coughing as the home she'd cherished burned around her.

"The princess!" someone shouted in Farsi. Terror seized her heart, but she didn't stop. She had to escape.

As she reached a large open window that led to the gardens, a dark figure stepped into her path. She ran into him, and he gripped her body with one arm and clamped a hand over her mouth.

"It's Al-Zahrani, my princess. I've come to rescue you. Come with me, quickly."

She followed him out of the window into the night.

Zehra shouted as she jolted upright. The night still held on to the world outside. Had she only been asleep an hour before the night-mare woke her?

Lawrence leapt from his chair by the fireplace, snatching a fire poker and wielding it like a saber. "What is it? What's the matter?" He seemed braced for a fight, legs spread in a crouched stance. Zehra's blood roared in her ears as she struggled to calm. No, she was not in Persia. She was safe. Wasn't she?

"I…" She swallowed thickly, her throat raw from the scream. "I had a bad dream."

Lawrence relaxed and walked over to the washstand by the bed. He poured her a glass of water from a pitcher next to the porcelain basin.

She accepted the glass, drinking deep until it was empty. Her body was covered in a sheen of sweat, and she lifted her hands, examining them for blood. She knew it wouldn't be there, but she felt it all the same.

"What are you looking for?" Lawrence filled her glass again.

"It's nothing. I'm so sorry I woke you," she whispered.

Lawrence leaned over the bed. She was surprised that she did not instinctively shy away from him.

"Sweetheart, something terrible has happened to you. I see it shadowing your eyes—there's a ghostly glimmer of pain behind them. But if you won't talk to me, I cannot help you." He cupped her face with one palm, and his warm hand felt so good against her skin. There was something about the way he touched her, spoke to her, as though he was too close, yet not close enough. She felt suddenly cold beneath the thin fabric of the chemise and longed for him to wrap his arms around her and warm her. It was madness, craving a stranger in this way, yet she did.

"Perhaps one day I can tell you," she said. "But not today."

His lips curved down into a frown, but he nodded. "I under-stand. Tell me what can I do. There must be something."

Zehra looked away from him, her eyes studying the plaster-work of the ceiling. Golden light, with painted roundels depicting scenes she recognized from classical mythology. She was more used to geometric patterns than depictions of people and was arrested by the sight of the art she saw above her now. Such beauty in the home of such a roguish bachelor. It was unexpected.

"Zehra?" He spoke her name with tenderness, and she finally met his gaze.

"Would you...hold me?" She knew it was improper, whether in England or in Persia, but being held was what she needed most. Whenever he touched her, the pain and fear of the past seemed to fade to a distant, hazy memory. She knew it was only a temporary solution, but she clutched at any chance, however small, to ease her memories and forget.

Lawrence's eyebrows rose. "Hold you? Are you quite sure?"

"Quite sure," she echoed.

"Er...right." He removed his boots, then eased down onto the bed beside her and opened his arms. Zehra was flooded with a rush of emotions as she slid into his embrace. She was asking so much of this man, a total stranger, and she could give him nothing in return. Her eyes filled with tears, and she buried her face against his chest. His scent enveloped her, and she relaxed almost immediately.

"Better?" he whispered. His warm breath fanned the crown of her hair.

"Yes." Zehra was silent a long moment. "I am not a weak woman." She wasn't sure why she needed him to hear her say that, but she did.

"I know, sweetheart. I think you may be the *strongest* woman I've ever met."

The tension in her body eased a little, and she let out a breath slowly. Could she share part of it with him? Perhaps a little...

"My parents were killed. I found them, their bodies, before I escaped from my home. It was..." There were no words, not ones strong enough to express her grief and pain.

His arms tightened around her. "My God. What happened? Why were they killed?"

Zehra curled her fingers into his shirt, desperate to hold onto him.

"My father stood in the way of a power-hungry man, someone he trusted. That man betrayed us to help another shah take our land. That is why I cannot go back." It was all she could say. If she breathed Al-Zahrani's name, made that threat in the gardens a reality, it could never be unsaid. It was better if Lawrence never knew of the danger. He might seek Al-Zahrani out, and that would get him killed because Lawrence was a man of honor and Al-Zahrani was not.

Lawrence stroked her hair with a soothing caress. "You're safe with me. I swear to you." Lawrence's lips touched her forehead in a chaste kiss that seemed to string together parts of her broken heart. "Sleep. I'll hold you as long as you want."

"You're a wonderful man," she murmured, settling deeper into his arms as they both shifted to lie back on the bed.

He chuckled, the sound making her feel warm and relaxed. "If you ever perchance meet my mother, you'll have to tell her that. But I doubt she would believe you."

She smiled a little. "Meet your mother? Heavens, let's pray that never happens."

"Why not?" He asked, half teasing, half serious.

Zehra nuzzled his chest. "Because she will undoubtedly wish to know how we met, and you will have to say, 'Mother, she is my slave, I bought her at the most dreadful brothel for seven thousand pounds.' I fear she would drop dead on the spot from such news." She chuckled a little despite herself.

"Yes, well, I suspect learning I'd spent seven thousand pounds on anything might do that."

"And not the part about owning a slave?" she teased.

Lawrence growled a little. "You are not my slave, Zehra. You're free to come and go as you please. I only ask that you be safe. I can set you up in your own house, supply you with clothes, food, whatever you wish until we figure out what to do next." He cleared his throat. "I ask for nothing in return."

She found the slit in his shirt and rubbed her fingertips along his bare chest, enjoying how warm his skin was. She knew she was tempting him, but she couldn't seem to help herself. He was strong, warm, and utterly masculine. He made her feel feminine and safe in a way she hadn't in many weeks.

"You're killing me," he whispered.

"Am I?" she asked, smiling.

"Touch me anywhere else and I might not be able to stop from touching you back," he warned, but there was a tenderness in the threat that made her burn with new hungers, ones she'd never felt for a man before. "Think of my poor honor."

She continued to brush her fingers over his chest and buried her face in his shoulder. The feel of his arms around her and being tucked against his side was hypnotic. It was lulling her into sleep very, very slowly.

"Feeling better?" he asked.

She nodded.

"Good. Just remember, no nightmares can grow where sunlight blossoms."

"What?" she asked, waking a little. It sounded like something her father might have said.

"It was something my father always said to me as a boy." Lawrence chuckled. "He taught me to picture everything that frightened me as dark shadows and then to imagine that I carried a beam of sunlight in my hands, and I could shine that beam across the shadows, burning them away with the light."

Zehra took a moment to imagine her past horrors, which were already cloaked in shadows, and then cast sunlight upon them in her mind. She couldn't be sure if it worked, but she didn't feel quite as helpless as she had before. The darkness had given these visions power, and imagining the light had given her strength. She only hoped it was enough.

"You are a wonderful man."

Her rescuer brushed his knuckles across her cheek and let out a slow, deep breath, but he didn't speak. She smiled a little but couldn't ignore the lethargy creeping along her limbs as she fell into a blissful, dreamless sleep where she hoped nightmares could not follow.

His Wicked Embrace comes out March 5th 2018 as a standalone story! Grab it HERE!

Turn the page to see a list my other steamy romances!

OTHER TITLES BY LAUREN SMITH

Historical
The League of Rogues Series
Wicked Designs
His Wicked Seduction
Her Wicked Proposal
Wicked Rivals
Her Wicked Longing
His Wicked Embrace (coming soon)
The Earl of Pembroke (coming soon)
His Wicked Secret (coming soon)
The Seduction Series
The Duelist's Seduction
The Rakehell's Seduction
The Rogue's Seduction (coming soon)
Standalone Stories
Tempted by A Rogue
Sins and Scandals
An Earl By Any Other Name
A Gentleman Never Surrenders
A Scottish Lord for Christmas

Contemporary
The Surrender Series
The Gilded Cuff
The Gilded Cage
The Gilded Chain
Her British Stepbrother
Forbidden: Her British Stepbrother
Seduction: Her British Stepbrother
Climax: Her British Stepbrother

Paranormal
Dark Seductions Series
The Shadows of Stormclyffe Hall
The Love Bites Series
The Bite of Winter
Brotherhood of the Blood Moon Series
Blood Moon on the Rise (coming soon)
Brothers of Ash and Fire
Grigori: A Royal Dragon Romance
Mikhail: A Royal Dragon Romance (coming soon)
Rurik: A Royal Dragon Romance (coming soon)

Sci-Fi Romance
Cyborg Genesis Series
Across the Stars (coming soon)

ABOUT THE AUTHOR

Lauren Smith is an Oklahoma attorney by day, author by night who pens adventurous and edgy romance stories by the light of her smart phone flashlight app. She knew she was destined to be a romance writer when she attempted to re-write the entire *Titanic* movie just to save Jack from drowning. Connecting with readers by writing emotionally moving, realistic and sexy romances no matter what time period is her passion. She's won multiple awards in several romance subgenres including: New England Reader's Choice Awards, Greater Detroit BookSeller's Best Awards, and a Semi-Finalist award for the Mary Wollstonecraft Shelley Award.

To connect with Lauren, visit her at:
www.laurensmithbooks.com
lauren@Laurensmithbooks.com

ABOUT THE ARTIST

Over the last twenty plus years Teresa Sprekelmeyer been designing everything from web sites to marketing graphics for clients who range from Hair stylists to Hollywood studios, with a great deal in between.

Needing a change, Teresa decided to shift her focus to something that she has a private passion for...romance novels.

With each cover she create, she hopes that her passion comes through to the author who decides to use is and to the readers that love these stories as much as she does!

*Teresa's art is featured throughout the book during scenes of passion.

To learn about Teresa's art visit:

http://midnightmusedesigns.com/website/

ABOUT THE ILLUSTRATOR

J oanne Renaud, who earned a BFA in illustration from Art Center College of Design, has been writing, drawing and painting as long as she can remember. She went to college in a variety of places, including Northern Ireland and Southern California, and enjoys history, comics, children's books, and cheesy fantasy movies from the '80s. She currently works as both an author and a freelance illustrator in the Los Angeles area. Her novel "Doors" was released from Champagne Books in 2016, and her illustration clients include Simon & Schuster, Random House, Houghton Mifflin, Macmillan-McGraw Hill, Harcourt Inc., Scholastic, and Compass Media.

Website: http://www.joannerenaud.com/
DeviantArt: http://suburbanbeatnik.deviantart.com/
Tumblr: http://suburbanbeatnik.tumblr.com/
Facebook: http://www.facebook.com/joanne.renaud.7
Twitter: http://twitter.com/suburbanbeatnik